by the same author

TRINA FINDS A BROTHER

LITTLE SISTER TAI-MI

TORRIS, THE BOY
FROM BROAD VALLEY

TORRIS, THE BOY
FROM BROAD VALLEY

by Berit Braenne

Translated from the Norwegian by
Lise Sømme McKinnon

Illustrated by Borghild Rud

Harcourt Brace Jovanovich, Inc., New York

FIRST AMERICAN EDITION

Originally published in Norway in 1967 by H. Aschehoug & Co. under the
title of *Tørris gutten fra Storlidalen*

ISBN 0-15-289489-6

Library of Congress Catalog Card Number: 79-124841

PRINTED IN THE UNITED STATES OF AMERICA

Contents

	THE HISTORY OF BARD'S FARM	9
1	*Torris and Father Go to the Village*	11
2	*Torris Gets a Present*	21
3	*Lady Comes Home*	44
4	*Bear Abroad on the Hill*	54
5	*Mountain Wind*	64
6	*Lady and Her Friend from the Wood*	97
7	*Mikkelina Gets into Deep Water*	104
8	*The Great Storm*	117
9	*Torris Follows Animal Tracks*	132
10	*Bogga Finds a Red Mitten*	140
11	*And It Came to Pass*	149

TORRIS, THE BOY
FROM BROAD VALLEY

The History of Bard's Farm

Once, many hundreds of years ago, a man came wandering from the east in among the mountains of Trollheimen. He was the first Bard, Torris's great-great-great-grandfather.

Among the wild mountains he found a pleasant valley with broad hilly slopes and a large and beautiful lake full of fish. There he settled and started to build. He called his farm Vasli, which means "the farm near the lake."

Later on, his eldest son extended the farm, cleared the forest, and tilled more earth, and his grandson continued the work. In this way Bard's Farm, as it came to be called, grew larger and better with each new generation.

By Torris's time—1848—it had become a good place to live, but there was still some wild country in Broad Valley. Elk and beasts of prey lived in the huge forests, bears padded about the moors, and the people of the mountains had to manage as best they could, living close to wild animals and savage nature.

By now many more farms have appeared in the valley,

and there is electricity and telephones; and there are roads and tractors and a milk truck that drives up and down every day.

But Bard's Farm, which has become a large and grand place, still lies where it lay when Bard started to build. Still the wild beasts roam the forests, still the avalanches thunder down the mountainsides, and still new little boys and girls grow up and play on the slopes by the clear water.

Therefore, this book is dedicated to:
The children at Bard's Farm.

Some names of places and persons in the book I have invented, and the Black Gorge does not exist any longer. But Broad Valley and Bard's Farm you will find if you ever walk the mountains of Trollheimen.

BERIT BRAENNE

1

Torris and Father Go to the Village

It was early morning when Torris awakened. He knew it because the sun had barely risen above the mountain. It shone in low through the small window in his bed closet, and he arose quietly. He did not want to waken Bard, who shared his bunk. His little brother still slept soundly with one arm above his head.

Grandfather's and Grandmother's bunk along the opposite wall stood empty. All the grownups were out of bed.

Torris slipped into the kitchen, where a fire was already burning in the hearth. Grandmother had gone to the cow barn, but Mother was there. She sat on a low stool with Little Marit in her lap.

"Good morning, Torris," she said, and looked at him.

Then she smiled. Every morning she smiled like that, as if she was equally glad to see him every new day.

Torris walked up to her and butted his forehead against her hair. It smelled so nice, and he thought she was so pretty, with bare arms and the bodice tucked into her skirt.

But then an important thought struck him.

"Where's Father?" he asked, and ran to the window. "He hasn't gone without me, has he?"

"No, he certainly hasn't!" said Mother. "He and Grandpa are down in the stable getting Blakken ready. He must look nice when you're going to the village. Hurry up and wash yourself and get your clothes on. I have laid out what you're going to wear."

Torris hurried as fast as he could.

But it took some time this morning because he wanted to look his very best. He had to try to scrub his hands clean, and that was not easy when he had been picking potatoes and digging in the earth three days running. He even ran down to the brook and washed his feet.

Grandmother came up from the cow barn with the milk pails just then.

"Good morning, Torris! Aren't you quite well today?" she asked, and stopped.

"Of course I am. Why?" Torris asked.

Grandmother laughed. "It's not like you to wash your feet *that* often. You washed them no later than last night."

"Yes, but I've been working in the field so much that it is almost impossible to get them clean," Torris said. He took another handful of sand and scrubbed till his feet glowed bright red.

"That's surely enough," Grandmother said. "Remember, your toes don't show through stockings and shoes."

Ow, he had forgotten that. He was going to wear stock-

ings and shoes today. Normally he ran barefoot all summer, but going to the village was different.

In a flash he was across the yard and up the steps. He nearly stumbled over pussy, who was on her way out at the same time, and he skipped past her on one foot.

"Can I eat now?" he called.

"Hush! Don't waken Little Marit. She is about to sleep

again," Mother said. "It will be good if she'll take another little nap while I make the porridge."

She hung the pot on the iron hook and swung it in over the fire.

Meanwhile, Torris went across and looked into the cradle. Funny having a little sister like this. When he saw her first, just after she was born, he could hardly believe that anything so small existed. Such tiny little fingers, and toes like pink peas! But it was strange how quickly she developed. When he reached his hand down to her now, she grasped one of his fingers hard, and she had such a firm grip that he had to loosen her hand to get free.

"Today we're going to the minister to see about a day for your christening," he said softly.

Little Marit blinked sleepily.

"It is an important errand, you see," he continued. "Grandma doesn't need to make fun of me because I wash myself, because many things may happen on such an outing."

Little Marit opened her blue eyes and looked into his.

He rocked her slowly while he chatted. The cradle stood close by Mother's and Father's bunk. She lay there snugly, well up from the draft on the floor, where Mother had only to stretch out her arm to rock her if she cried during the night.

Now she was asleep. Torris tiptoed carefully away and dressed himself.

The porridge was ready, and they sat down around the long table.

Bard came paddling along, rubbing sleep out of his eyes. He was always the last one to awaken. His cheeks were warm and red, and Grandmother took him up on her lap.

"We'll dress you afterward," she said. "Now we'll have to eat so that Father and Torris can get off."

"May I come, too?" Bard asked.

"You'd better wait till next time," Father said. "It's not so easy to have more than two on the horse, you know."

"When I am grown up, I'll build a road right up to Bard's Farm so that we can drive with a cart," Torris said.

"Ho, ho." Grandfather laughed. "Then you'll have plenty to do, Torris."

"Yes, there will have to be more people here in Broad Valley before we have a road," Father said. "Many men are needed for a job like that, even if they work at it for many years."

Torris thought about it. Father and Grandfather were probably right. There were only two farms up here, Bard's Farm and Saeter, and only four grown-up men in the whole valley. Down in the main valley there were lots of farms and crofts and lots of men. No wonder they had fine roads there.

But shortly afterward, when Torris was sitting behind Father on Blakken's broad back, he was rather pleased that they had no road. Nothing was better than to sit rocking on the horse's back, listening and watching. The carts in the village rumbled so horribly that it was impossible to hear anything, and they went so fast that scarcely anything could be seen either.

When he and Father rode like this, on the soft forest carpet, they could hear all the sounds from the forest and look around as much as they wished.

Down in Bard's Lake the shiny trout jumped, making lovely widening rings. Now and then a hare came leaping across the path, and they occasionally saw an elk, too, when Blakken ambled gently along, like today. The thought of what they might meet around the next bend in the dense undergrowth was always exciting, and Torris was alert to every sound and to everything that moved.

Blakken jogged along without Father's having to talk to him. The horse knew well this path that humans and animals had trodden during many hundreds of years. It ran along the edge of Bard's Lake, out and in through pines and birches. All they had to do was to follow it.

But halfway along the lake the path divided. One branch went to Saeter, while the other continued alongside the lake, and here Blakken stopped and turned his head, as if asking, "Where do you want to go today?"

"We'll take the path by the lake, Blakken," Father said, and gently pulled the reins.

Blakken trotted on, out of the forest and across the fields below Saeter.

In a newly cleared field above the path a boy and an old man were working. It was Little John and his grandfather, Old John. Father stopped Blakken and talked for a time to the old man, while Torris watched Little John, who was picking up stones and throwing them in a heap. From time to time he took up a small stone with his bare toes and tossed it onto the pile. He hit his target most of the time.

Torris would gladly have jumped down from Blakken and had a go at it himself. But of course he had his shoes on, so it couldn't be done.

"We're going to the village," he said.

"You're lucky," said Little John. He would much rather have gone along to the village than work here with his old grandfather, who almost never spoke a word.

It wasn't that Old John was in any way angry or bad. He was just a little bit sullen and rough, and when he spoke, he seemed to bark. He certainly wasn't entertaining, nor did he say much on this occasion, so Father and Torris were soon on their way again.

"Poor Little John having such a sour grandpa," said Torris when they had gone a little way.

"Well, yes, but he is a very hard worker, and nobody can touch him as a hunter," said Father.

They swung along the southern end of the lake. The morning mist still lay over the blue-green water, and Torris shivered slightly.

"You'd better run for a bit and get yourself warm," Father said.

Torris jumped down from Blakken and ran on ahead. He was not used to running with shoes on, so he stopped, took off both shoes and stockings, and handed them to Father. It didn't matter if he ran barefoot here on the clean track. Blakken pushed impatiently at his back with his soft muzzle.

"All right, we are going now." Torris laughed and ruffled his mane. And the horse took a hold of the boy's hair and tugged gently at it. It was a game they played.

"Shall we race one another?" cried Torris, and shot off along the track.

Blakken whinnied and jogged after him. They ran in this way till they reached the edge of the wood, where it opened out toward the broad valley. Here a brook ran across the path. The water gushed cold and clear over the stones, and Torris lay on his stomach and took a drink.

Blakken stopped, too. He lowered his big head beside

the boy and took a long drink. When he lifted his head, the water dripped from his muzzle down on to Torris's neck.

"Oh, Blakken, don't!" Torris laughed and rolled over onto his back.

He stretched his arms right out in the moss and stared out over the valley and up toward the sky. It was clear and pale blue. Through the red and gold autumn leaves he saw all the mountaintops around Bard's Lake. Snow was lying on the highest peaks, and it gleamed pink on the slopes facing the morning sun, while all the slopes in the shade were light blue.

Torris stared right around the skyline, and it seemed to him that he was lying at the bottom of a huge bowl and that the mountains were the rim of the bowl. The sky was so far away that he became dizzy and had to shut his eyes. But when he opened them again, his gaze met a dark dot right above Bard's Ridge. It was a great bird circling around. It didn't move its wings and didn't make a sound —just swept around in mighty arcs.

Torris sat up.

"Look at that big bird, Father," he said.

Father shaded his eyes.

"It's the golden eagle," he said.

"Oh! The golden eagle! How big is it?"

Father stretched out both his arms. "It's as big as *this* between its wing tips, and we can add one of your arms, too."

"Then it's huge all right," said Torris, and stared at the bird once more.

Suppose he could have floated like that high above the

mountains and seen everything from above. How wonderful it would have been!

He stretched out his arms and ran as fast as he could— he turned and flew around in wide circles and tried to feel like an eagle. But it was difficult as long as he had to keep his feet on the ground, and he kept stumbling in the clumps of heather as well.

Finally he gave up and ran back to Father, who lifted him up onto Blakken again. Come to think of it, it was just as fine to be a boy on a horse.

They rode at a brisk trot through the valley. The heather was purple with tufts of white bog cotton in between, and they scared two ptarmigan, which flew off cackling toward the brush. Then Blakken rounded the end of Bard's Lake and made off downward beside the river.

It flowed wide and smooth for a bit. But soon the valley narrowed, and they came down through Black Gorge, where the current ran faster and the path was steeper. Here both Torris and Father dismounted and walked. The path was stony, and Blakken placed his feet carefully so as not to stumble.

Black Gorge was always in the shade. Torris thought it was an eerie place and kept close behind Father.

On one side, the mountain rose so steeply that he had to put his head right back to see the top. On the other side, the waterfall roared and thundered so much that he and Father had to shout to hear each other. A thin, misty spray fell on his face, and the path was slippery under his feet.

"We'll soon be down," cried Father, turning his head.

Torris nodded. He wasn't exactly afraid. He had walked

here before with Father and Mother and knew the way.
He just didn't like to have that closed-in feeling.

Father halted again, pointing upward.

"There's loose rock here," he shouted. "Some time or
other a good bit of it is going to come down, maybe in two
years, maybe a hundred. But then it'll be broader and
clearer here in Black Gorge. Perhaps you will be the one
who'll level out a new path."

Torris smiled and wished that it might happen while he
was alive.

Then they reached the place where the mountain
veered off and the path swung away from the waterfall.
They stood on a bare knoll, from which they could see the
whole village with all the farms and the road that wound
its way along to the church and the manse.

Torris felt himself prickling with excitement. Something
strange and unusual always happened when they were in
the village.

"We shan't waste time in getting there," said Father,
and lifted him up onto Blakken once again.

2

Torris Gets a Present

Father and Torris soon came to the first big farm, where
the road began, and from here Blakken didn't need much
time to reach the manse gate. A servant came running to
open it and, when they dismounted, took the horse into
the stable. Torris hurried to get his stockings and shoes on
and followed Father.

Oh, what a farm!

It took Torris's breath away every time he came here.

Apart from the huge main building itself, there must
have been at least fifteen outbuildings of all shapes and
sizes. There were cow barns and stables and a storehouse
on stilts—to keep the mice out; servants' quarters and a
carpenter's shed and a house for the old people; a wagon
shed and washhouse and a small building for steam bathing, and a whole mass of small houses besides. All were
made of solid timber and had green turf roofs, and the
manse itself had a splendid porch along the front.

Nonetheless, Torris thought that the finest of all was a

tiny little house that stood at the foot of the garden. It was
built like the storehouse on stilts with two small windows
and was a playhouse for keeping toys. He would love to
have seen inside it if he had dared to ask. It belonged to
the minister's youngest daughter.

But Father was now making his way through the farm,
and Torris hurried along after him. He caught up with him
again by the wide stone stairway at the main door, and
they were just about to walk up it when a man came at full
speed along the porch. It was the minister. He was in such
a rush that he very nearly knocked Father down.

"Good day!" Father greeted him.

"Oh, it's you, is it, Bard Estenson!" exclaimed the minister, and halted. His wig hung at an angle over one ear.
"How are things in Broad Valley?"

"Very well, thank you," said Father. "And all is well
with you people here, I hope?"

"Yes, thank you," said the minister. "It's just that our
sheep have vanished. The servants have been up in the
hills for two days searching for them, but they can't find
them anywhere."

"That's bad," Father said.

"Yes, especially if there's been a bear about!" said the
minister.

Torris moved closer in alarm and then stared from the
minister to Father.

A bear? Oh, please, no! They still had some of their
sheep up on the mountain, too, and Torris had his own
lamb there—Little Maid. Just suppose the bear had gotten
hold of Little Maid!

Father shook his head. There were bears on the mountain, true enough, but he hadn't heard that there was a killer about, he said.

"But where can the sheep have gone?" the minister asked, with arms outstretched.

"Maybe they've wandered off to our side," suggested Father. "We are going to get in the rest of our own animals tomorrow, and we can look out for yours at the same time."

This pleased the minister. He didn't trust his own servants very far; they were not much good at looking for sheep, he said. Then he straightened his wig a little and invited Father and Torris in.

He went ahead of them along the long porch to his study. Torris trotted behind them, thinking about Little Maid. He could not get the bear out of his mind. And as he was about to step through the doorway, he failed to notice the high threshold and so fell flat on his face, sprawling full length on the floor.

The minister turned around and looked at him in astonishment.

"Are you looking for something?" he inquired.

"No—ah—oh, no," stammered Torris. "I was just thinking about Little Maid."

"About Little Maid? Have you already got a sweetheart at your age?" asked the minister.

Torris did not reply. He felt himself turning red. Imagine the minister thinking that Little Maid was a girl. How silly!

But he had no chance to explain who Little Maid was, for the minister was already sitting at his desk.

"Well, now, what business have you come on, Bard Estenson?" he inquired.

Father unbuttoned his jacket.

"I should like to have my young daughter christened before winter comes to the hills," he said.

"That is wise," said the minister, and took out an enormous book. "If it suits you, we might say the Sunday after next. And what is the child to be called?"

"She is to be called Marit," said Father.

"Right," said the minister, and took the long quill pen from the inkstand. "Marit Bardsdatter—er—?

"Vasli," said Father. "Marit Bardsdatter Vasli."

The minister leaned back in his leather upholstered chair and looked at Father.

"Why is your farm called Vasli when the valley is called Broad Valley?" he asked.

"Well, Great-Great-Grandfather Bard was responsible for that," explained Father. "When he came to the valley, he called it Broad Valley because it had such fine broad meadows, but he called the farm Vasli, which means 'the farm near the lake.' Most people nowadays just call it Bard's Farm."

The minister nodded and lit his long-stemmed pipe. He drew on it and looked out of the window. "Old Bard was an able fellow, they tell me."

"Yes, indeed," said Father. "They say he was a fine wood-carver and wrought-iron worker and clever at building houses."

"You have a good inheritance." The minister nodded and dipped his pen again.

He wrote for some time with large curly letters, both Father's name and Mother's name and a good deal besides. Torris stood away over beside the door, thinking about Little Maid and sweating. It was very warm in the study, and the minister seemed to feel it warm as well, for he suddenly took off his wig and placed it on the table.

Torris stared at him with amazement.

Without his wig he just looked like any ordinary man. Torris had thought the minister had no hair of his own and was quite old. But now he looked much younger. His hair was dark, rather like Father's, and if it had not been for his fine clothes, he might almost have resembled the merchant in the general store. It was a fantastic change. It was as if Blakken had changed into an elk . . .

The minister had now finished writing and closed the book. As he looked up, his eye fell on Torris.

"And what is your name?" he asked in friendly tones.

Torris could scarcely help grinning. The minister had asked the same question twice before, each time they had visited the manse.

"My name is Torris Bardson Vasli," he replied.

"Yes, yes, so it is, of course," said the minister. "You'll inherit Bard's Farm after your father, I suppose?"

"That is the idea, yes," Father replied for him.

The minister nodded.

"When you are grown up and are going to marry Little Maid, you'll invite me to the wedding at Bard's Farm, won't you?" he said as he stood up.

Father glanced at Torris and smiled. But Torris felt his cheeks blazing all over again. He was more than happy when the two grownups left the study. It would be fine to get some air. He hurried after them, and this time he took a big jump over the high threshold. At least he would not trip over it again.

This seemed destined to be his unlucky day, though, for just at that moment one of the girls came out of the

kitchen with a large keg of flour in her arms, and Torris
was going so fast that he bumped his head on the keg from
underneath, making it jump into the air. The girl yelled,
the flour rose like a cloud about them, and the keg rolled
like a barrel hoop along the porch.

"What are you up to, boy?" Father called.

Torris did not manage to answer. He lay flat and puffed
out flour while he stared up in despair at the minister. But
the minister only laughed.

"What a fight you are having with that threshold," he
said. "Go along with Beret, and she'll brush you down.
And you, Bard Estenson, must come along with me to the
stable and see my new horse."

Father was delighted to do this, and the two men
walked down through the farm chatting, while Torris
trudged after Beret along the porch. He felt just like a
puppy that has done something wrong, and he wished he
was in the depths of the darkest corner. That such a thing
should happen here in the manse! And to him, when he
had been looking forward so much to the visit!

Beret asked him to wait and came back immediately
with a huge broom. "Take your jacket off and turn
around," she said.

Torris looked at her in alarm. Was she going to beat
him?

But she just laughed and brushed off his jacket and trousers.

"What a sight you are!" She laughed. "Take off your
shoes and stockings and give them a good shaking."

Torris did as she asked and was more than glad that he
had washed himself so well. It was easy to see he had. You
never knew what could happen when you went to the vil-

lage. He placed his sand-scoured feet confidently down on the floor and beat and shook for all he was worth. His clothes were soon as fine as before.

While he was dressing, the minister's wife came out on the porch. She was small and neat and gentle and always looked as if she were a little shy.

"Good day, Torris," she said in her soft, friendly voice. "Have you seen my husband?"

"Yes, he's in the stable along with Father," replied Torris.

"Oh, yes." The minister's wife nodded. "Thank you."

She leaned against one of the large pillars, and Torris looked at her. She was the loveliest lady he knew, next to Mother. And then she always remembered his name. Not all grownups did that . . .

Just then Father and the minister came out of the stable with the new horse, a beautiful white mare. They admired her from every side, and the minister's wife waited a while.

Then she called gently, "Nicolas, food is ready. Please come in and eat now and bring your guest with you."

Father looked up and bowed his thanks, and the minister, taking his eyes away from the horse an instant, nodded vaguely.

"Ah—uh, thanks, my dear!" he said, and went on admiring the fine animal. He obviously hadn't heard anything and had no idea what he was replying to. Nor did he give any appearance of coming.

The minister's wife smiled slightly and waited. Then she called again that the food was waiting.

"Ah, yes, right," mumbled the minister.

He was now standing with his head almost in the horse's mouth, examining the animal's teeth. It was quite clear that he was just answering automatically out of the blue. Father shifted from one foot to the other, looking somewhat ill at ease. He would have preferred to be polite and come when the minister's wife invited him, but quite obviously he couldn't go before the minister went.

Torris swallowed. This was getting serious. Perhaps they wouldn't get any food at the manse today at all.

Then another woman came out on the porch. She was large and stately, with round red cheeks and a huge white apron over her skirt. Torris knew her well. This was Bogga, the minister's cook. She took up her position beside the minister's wife, with arms akimbo, and looked out over the farmyard, like a captain surveying his command.

"Minister!" she yelled. "Food's out!"

Then the minister's head came out of the horse's mouth quickly enough.

"Eh—what—food?" he said, and blinked his eyes. It looked exactly as if he had been newly awakened by a bucket of cold water.

"Yes, food." Bogga repeated loudly. "And if the minister doesn't want his meat cold, he'd better come at once!"

The minister looked at Father somewhat bewildered. He mumbled something or other about having another look at the horse later. Then he gripped it by the mane and hurried down to the stable, where the servant came and took the animal.

Bogga stood waiting all this time. She did not go before she saw the two men coming. Then she nodded and followed the minister's wife.

"We managed that fine," she said.

The minister's wife turned and smiled at Bogga, and Bogga turned and winked at Torris.

"It sometimes happens, you see, that the minister is a little hard of hearing, especially when he's talking about his horses."

And so they were all finally seated around the long table in the huge kitchen, Father, Torris, and the entire household of the manse.

And what a household it was!

Besides the minister's own family, the three children and the old parents, there were two servants, two housemaids, two kitchen maids, a dairymaid and the two girls that helped her, and lastly some old paupers and two little children that Torris did not know. It was like a whole party seated around the long table. Torris completely forgot to eat, with so much to look at and figure out.

The minister's family sat at the top end of the table, and right opposite Torris sat the minister's youngest daughter, the one who owned the playhouse at the foot of the garden. She was called Gunhild. She had two long braids bound together with a blue ribbon low down her back, and she had two big blue eyes that looked across at Torris.

Torris stared back. He couldn't prevent himself. He wondered if Little Marit would be just as pretty when she grew up.

Suddenly Bogga was behind him ruffling his hair.

"Are you not going to eat, Torris," she said, "or will I have to feed you?"

Torris looked up at her in annoyance. Imagine saying such a thing when all the others were sitting around listening. Gunhild had certainly heard it as well, even if she was kind and didn't laugh.

But then Bogga bent over and said softly in his ear, "You'll have to come along to the cow barn afterward, and you'll see something you'll like."

"What is it?" whispered Torris.

"Wait and see," said Bogga. She put a fresh meatball on his plate, and Torris ate slowly, wondering what exciting thing it could be that Bogga had in the byre. Kittens? Yes, that's what it would be. He looked forward with joy to seeing them, and as soon as they were finished eating, he sat down on the box of firewood and waited for Bogga.

Gunhild stood over by the door and peeped at him. But when he looked at her, she ran out. He would have liked to follow her and see if she went down to her playhouse. But it was even more exciting to see what Bogga had in the byre, so he stayed where he was.

Little by little the kitchen emptied. They all returned to their tasks.

Father and the minister went down to the stable again to have another look at the white mare, the maids went to the well for water, and Bogga was busy cleaning up the kitchen. Torris looked at her as she walked to and fro, clearing away the food and wiping off the table.

Bogga was very special—she feared no one and nothing. She talked to the minister as if he were a little boy, and it was said that she had once caught an angry bull by the nostrils and held it firmly, while the farm servants ran for their lives and hid themselves. Bogga herself just pooh-poohed the story, but it was supposed to be true. She was as brave as the bravest man.

But she was kind and tenderhearted, too. She would not allow anyone to harm an animal. God help anyone who struck a horse or a dog if Bogga was around, for he would receive the same treatment from the broom handle as he had given the animal.

And Bogga had a most remarkable way with children, at least once they got to know her.

Torris sat wondering why she didn't have any children herself. And before he had time to think he blurted out, "Have you any children, Bogga?"

Bogga looked at him for a moment. Then she turned to the hearth and hung a cauldron of water over the fire.

"No," she said.

Torris looked at her back. It was broad and strong. Bogga looked as if she might easily have had ten children, and she would certainly have been good to them. And yet she had none.

He felt that he should not have asked her.

"But anyway you've got all the people in the manse here to look after," he said comfortingly, to make it up.

"Yes, you're right there, Torris," said Bogga, turning around and laughing. "The minister and his wife and the maids and the servants and the whole shebang, and they're all of them just big children in their own ways, including the minister."

Torris laughed, both because she called the minister a child and because he was glad that Bogga laughed.

"Yes, and you've also got Sissi and your birds," he said eagerly.

"I have that." Bogga nodded. "Animals are the best friends you can have. They are loyal to you until they die. That's more than you can say for many people."

"But angry bulls and dangerous bears?" inquired Torris.

"Oh, yes," said Bogga. "A bull may well get angry because it's been penned in for too long, and a bear can get sour when he's old and stiff and having trouble finding food. But come along now. We'll go and say hello to someone who's neither sour nor dangerous."

Torris leaped to his feet.

Bogga filled a bowl with milk and went on ahead, and he ran after her down through the farm. On a bench by the sunny wall sat the old paupers taking their rest, and the small children, a boy and a girl, lay on the grass playing with some pine cones.

Bogga stopped for a moment. She put her hand in her pocket and fished out two cookies, which she gave to the children. They took them but said nothing. They only stared with wondering eyes at the big, strong cook.

"Poor little things," said Bogga when they had passed on. "They're not used to getting anything unless they beg for it."

Torris knew that.

Paupers were old folk and little ones who had been left alone in the world and couldn't fend for themselves. So they lived by turns in the big farms, a few weeks here and a few weeks there, and they weren't equally well received everywhere. In some places they had to sleep in the cow barn or in the hayloft and were chased out to beg for the food they needed.

No wonder these children looked frightened.

Torris looked back at them and then up at Bogga. A thought suddenly struck him.

"Couldn't you have a child like that and be its mother?" he asked. "I mean—keeping it all the time."

Bogga stopped. She looked in surprise at Torris.

"It's strange you should say that, for I've thought of it

myself," she said after a time. "If I only knew that Mr. Nicolas would remain here as minister in the manse, I'd have asked if I could have the little girl with me. There's plenty of room here and any amount of food."

"Do it!" said Torris. "Do it, Bogga! Nobody can cook like you—they all say so. Even if a new minister comes, he can't put you out."

"Hm," said Bogga thoughtfully, and walked on.

But she said no more, and Torris knew he shouldn't keep on talking about it any more just now.

It was dim and chilly in the cow barn. After the sharp light outside, the eyes needed time to get used to the half-dark, but Bogga walked at ease past all the empty stalls, and Torris followed close on her heels.

The cow barn was not, however, quite empty.

Torris caught sight of a massive brown back, and a huge head turned slowly toward them. It was the big bull. He stamped heavily with one of his hind legs, and a bellow came from deep down in his throat when Bogga stopped a moment and scratched him between the horns.

And there—two green eyes were shining toward him. It was the barn cat sitting on a log, licking itself.

"Are there many kittens?" asked Torris.

"Kittens?" said Bogga. "Who said there are kittens?"

"Isn't that what it is?" asked Torris. He could not see what else it might be.

"Look over here," Bogga said, leading the way toward one of the calf pens at the very end of the barn. The little door into the pen was ajar, and she pushed it right open.

"Take a peek!"

Torris tiptoed in.

There was a tiny window in the wall above the pen, and a sunbeam slanted down to a heap of straw and some ragged sacks. He squatted down and looked around. Something small was stirring there. A snout poked out, and another, and yet another. Dark blue eyes, round as marbles, stared at Torris. Wet black snouts sniffed the air. "Wuff!" they went, and five tubby little creatures struggled out of the straw and came rolling out onto the floor.

"Oh, it's puppies!" Torris cried.

"Sure, they're puppies." Bogga laughed. She lifted one of them up, and it licked her nose with lots of quick little licks, and wriggled its entire body from the tiny restless head to the tip of its tail.

"Easy, now, I've had a wash today already." She laughed and put it down.

"May I hold one?" Torris asked.

"Of course," said Bogga. "As long as you sit down, there's no risk that it'll hurt itself if it wriggles away from you."

It was not difficult for Torris to get hold of one. The puppies all tumbled around him, tripping and jumping up on him, wanting to find out what he was like. One of them bit hard on his sleeve and tugged and pulled; another caught sight of one of his shoes and began to growl and bark at it, as if it were a dangerous enemy.

Bogga sat down on a milking stool while Torris lifted up all the pups in turn and patted the warm round bodies. He couldn't tell which of them he liked best.

But one little one was rather more cautious than the others.

When it had sniffed Torris, it waddled a few steps backward and sat down on its tail, watching him. It had just the same shiny dark eyes as all the others and was just as nice and plump, but it was a bit smaller, and its coat was a shade lighter. Torris looked at it and stretched out his hand.

"Come on, then," he said.

The puppy cocked its head and pricked up one of its ears slightly.

"That's it—come on!" wheedled Torris again.

Then the pup got up and wriggled over to Torris. It raised its snout in the air, flattened its ears, and made itself so friendly, oh, so friendly. Its round little tummy almost swept the floor, and it lifted its paws up high at each step, as if it were afraid of tripping, even though there was nothing to trip over. In this way it reached Torris at last, and he lifted it up carefully and held it close to him.

"Do you like it?" Bogga asked.

"Yes," said Torris, "oh, yes!"

"It's a little lady," said Bogga. "All the other pups are male, but you can see that this one is more careful."

Yes, it was indeed.

Torris held it out and looked into its face, and the pup looked shyly sideways, so that the whites of its eyes showed. Torris had never seen anything quite so pretty. He held it close to him once more and placed his cheek against the smooth, round head.

Bogga sat looking at them for a while.

"Would you like it?" she inquired suddenly.

"Uh?" said Torris.

"I'm asking you if you'd like it," said Bogga.

Torris gaped. He stared from the pup to Bogga. He could hardly believe it—that he should get this pup to take with him, home to Bard's Farm, to keep forever.

If he'd like it!

When he was small, they had had a dog, but it was old and had died. They had often talked since then of getting a new one, but nothing had come of it. Father had said Bard and he were too small and careless to have a pup.

But now perhaps?

He set the pup down and got up quickly.

"I'll have to ask Father," he said. "Do you think he's in the stable?"

"He'll be there all right," said Bogga. "Just run."

Torris dashed off. He ran through the farm and into the stable, where Father and the minister were still standing examining the white mare.

"Father!" He yelled so loudly that the walls rang. "Can I have a pup?"

The white mare and the two other horses in the stable started when he yelled. They threw up their heads, pulling on their halters. The white mare, who was not tied, reared up on her hind legs and lashed out with her hoofs. The minister grasped her mane and held on firmly.

"What on earth are you doing, boy," called Father.

Torris stopped in alarm. He waited until the minister had calmed the horse.

"Now what was it?" asked Father.

"Well, eh, it's Bogga. She says I, eh . . ."

"Does Bogga want to give you a pup, is that it?" the minister asked kindly.

"Yes," Torris said, taking heart again and looking gratefully at the minister.

"Let me hear more about this," Father said. "I cannot reply before I know what I'm replying to."

Torris explained in a great rush about the five puppies and the little bitch that Bogga wished him to have.

"You must come and see it, Father!" he pleaded.

"We'd better both come along," said the minister. "I'll just tie the horse."

"Shall I run on ahead?" Torris asked.

"Yes, off you go." Father nodded.

Torris raced back to Bogga. Sissi, the pups' mother, had come in while he was away. She was busy licking her little ones, and they leaped around her, whining and carrying on as if they hadn't seen her for a hundred years.

"Now, now, you mustn't plague your poor old mother so," said Bogga. She placed the bowl of milk down on the floor for them and patted Sissi. "Look, here's Torris, who's going to have one of your little ones," she chatted. "It'll be good for you to get some peace soon. Your puppies have grown so big and troublesome."

Sissi wagged her tail and sniffed Torris's hand. Then she lay down at Bogga's feet, and immediately afterward Father and the minister arrived.

"Is it really true that you want to give Torris one of those fine pups?" asked Father.

"Yes, I do," Bogga said. "It will have a good life at Bard's Farm, and Torris will take good care of it."

"Oh, yes, I really will!" Torris said, and pointed at the pup. "That's it, Father. Isn't it nice? May I?"

Father nodded. "It's a fine dog. If Bogga is kind enough to let you have it, then we can only say 'thank you.'"

He reached out his hand to Bogga, and it struck Torris that he himself had completely forgotten to thank her. He threw himself around Bogga's neck and almost knocked her off the stool. After that he threw himself down on the floor and stared at the pup. He thought he could never tire of looking at it.

"What are you going to call your puppy, then, Torris?" the minister inquired. "Little Maid, perhaps?" he said with a wink.

"No, that's my lamb," said Torris.

At last he had managed to explain to the minister who Little Maid was. No, but—what was he to call the puppy?

"Lady, maybe?" said Bogga. "She certainly is a little lady."

"Yes, Lady is fine!" Torris cried, and Father and the minister agreed.

"You are never cheated when you get something from Borghild Halvard's daughter," the minister said.

"Borghild?" said Torris, and looked up.

"Yes, that's what my real name is," Bogga said with a laugh. "But it will soon be just the minister who knows it, because he's seen it in the church register. Anyway, I've been called Bogga for as long as I can remember, and it's good enough for me."

"To me your name *is* Bogga," Torris said, "and I'd rather call you that."

"Yes, it does sound a good round sort of word, doesn't it?" said Bogga with a laugh.

But it was now time to be getting off home. Bogga went into the kitchen and prepared a basket in which they could carry the pup on the way back, and she told Father and Torris what it should have to eat. It was important that it should get the food it was used to, or it could get an upset stomach.

Gunhild came into the kitchen just as Bogga finished her lecture. She went over to Torris, twisting her long braid around one index finger.

"Would you like to see my playhouse?" she asked suddenly.

Torris did not know what to say. Just at the moment the puppy was even more important. He looked up at Father.

"I'm afraid it'll have to be another time, Gunhild," said Father. "You see, we'll have to be going now."

Torris nodded. "I'd love to see it when we come for the christening . . . if I may."

"Yes," said Gunhild gravely, and turned away her face. Perhaps she was sorry that he said no when she asked him. He hoped she was not angry.

She certainly wasn't, though, for she went and brought a little doll's blanket, which she laid in the pup's basket.

"That's for your pup," she said.

"Oh—thank you ever so much!" said Torris, over-whelmed.

Yes, it was just as he had thought: Gunhild was very kind—as well.

Then they said good-by to the minister's family and to Bogga and went on their way.

Torris sat up front on Blakken and held the basket, and Father sat behind holding the reins. They paid a quick call on the merchant and bought a little salt and sugar and chewing tobacco, and then made straight for home. The sun was still high in the sky as they reached Bard's Lake.

"We'll have to look in at Saeter," Father said. "I'll ask Old John to come along with us and look for the sheep."

He jumped down from Blakken and led him up the steep slope. As soon as they entered the farmyard, they found Old John over by the woodshed chopping wood. Little John was helping to stack it.

"Once again, God's blessing on your work," Father said.

"Hmph!" grunted Old John.

But he didn't turn—merely went on chopping so hard that the chips flew in a shower about his ears. His gray hair hung down over his shoulders, and each time he turned his head to pick up another log, his long beard swung into the air. He looked very much like a gnarled little dwarf.

"You've a lot of fine winter wood, I see," Father said after a time.

"Hmph!" mumbled Old John.

"And it's grand weather for getting it dry into the shed," said Father.

Old John did not reply. He didn't seem to hear what Father was saying at all.

"Well, I've just been at the minister's," Father continued. "His sheep are missing, and I said I'd have a search for them."

Old John remained standing for a moment with his ax poised. Torris could tell from his back that he was listening. Little John cast a quick glance from his grandfather over to Father. He, too, was waiting eagerly.

"Well," said Father at length. "I thought perhaps we might need some help. They're big moors to cover, and we don't know whereabouts the sheep have gone."

Old John drove the ax into the chopping block and turned around.

"Why did you not say so in the first place!" he barked. "When do we go?"

"I wouldn't mind going tomorrow," Father said. "I've got some sheep up there myself, and the snow might come soon on the hills."

"Yes, and maybe there's a bear up there now," Torris said quickly.

Old John fixed his sharp eyes on Torris.

"A bear! Where did you hear that?"

"The minister said so . . . and I have my lamb up there, Little Maid."

"We'll go early tomorrow," Old John decided. "I'll bring my gun and the dog."

"Woof!" came at this very moment from the basket where Lady had been lying asleep on the way. She had awakened with all the noise.

"What was that?" inquired Old John.

"It's this," replied Torris, and reached the basket down to Father. "I got it from Bogga, the minister's cook."

Father took the lid off the basket and let the pup out on the grass. Old John cocked his head and took a look at it; then he stretched out one foot and wriggled it a little.

"Grrr, woof, woof!" yapped the pup at Old John's boot, and leaped backward on stiff legs.

The old man nodded.

"It'll be a good one," he said. "It's got the wits to look after itself, and it's got courage—even if it is a bitch."

Torris sat up straight in the saddle and smiled happily. Old John wasn't so bad after all. He knew about many things, no doubt about that.

"Right, then we'll meet tomorrow," Father said. He put the pup back in the basket, handed it to Torris, and swung himself up on the horse. "I suppose we might as well take the boys along," he added.

"Yes," said Old John, "so long as they don't bother us."

Torris and Little John stole a glance at each other. This was more than they had dared hope—being allowed to join a sheep search!

"It's because your Father asked," whispered Little John. "I'd never have been allowed if I'd asked myself."

Little John's mother and father came out and greeted them briefly. The father was a tall, rather serious man, dark of skin; the mother was plump and smiling and called to them in a high-pitched, clear voice to come in for a moment.

"Thanks for the invitation, but we must be getting home now," Father said, "or they'll be thinking Torris and I have gone off and left them."

Little John's mother burst out in light ringing laughter. It was carried away in the clear autumn air and reechoed among the mountains, and Father waved his broad-brimmed hat as he guided Blakken out through the gate.

3

Lady Comes Home

Everyone at Bard's Farm was busy with his own work when they arrived back.

Grandfather was doing some job in the smithy; Mother and Grandmother were washing clothes in the stream, but they stopped working immediately when Father and Torris rode into the farmyard and came to hear the news from the village.

Torris hurried in ahead with his basket. He placed it down in the corner by the hearth and lifted the lid a little. The pup was asleep.

"What have you got there?" asked Bard, and came to have a look.

"Hush, don't say anything," whispered Torris. "It's a puppy, but I'm going to give the others a surprise. Sit down on the woodbox and don't say a thing."

Bard did as he was told, and shortly afterward the four grownups came in. They were chatting about the minister's white mare, and Torris gathered that Father hadn't said anything about the pup yet. He sat down beside Bard and kept an eye on the basket.

Grandmother glanced at them.

"What are you both looking so crafty about?" she asked.

"Noth-nothing at all," said Torris. But when she turned away, Bard and he nearly burst out laughing, for at that very moment the pup poked its head out of the basket, and then it tumbled out and scampered right over to Grandmother. Perhaps it thought that her swishing skirt looked exciting. At any rate, it took a firm hold of the hem with its teeth, and when Grandmother turned around, it swung around with her as if she'd been a merry-go-round.

"Oh, what's this?" cried Grandmother.

She felt something clinging to her and turned around to see what it was.

Swish! The puppy went swirling around again.

"Ow, what *have* I got here?" yelled Grandmother, and lifted up her skirt to her knees.

But then the pup let go and rolled along the floor.

"Eeeh, eeeh," it yelped.

Grandmother stared at it. Then she clapped her hands together.

"Oh, no, the poor little thing," she said, and ran and picked it up. "Where have you come from?"

"My goodness!" cried Mother, and she, too, clapped her hands together. "Whose is it?"

"It's ours!" cried Torris. "I got it from Bogga. Isn't it nice?"

"Yes, it certainly is," Grandmother said. And just imagine—I thought it was a little pixie hanging onto my skirt."

They all admired it. Mother and Bard took turns in

holding it, hugging and patting it, and Grandfather took it in his huge hands and cradled it as if it were a human child.

"This little pup is a real beauty," he said happily.

"It's all right that we've got it, Mother? You don't mind?" Torris asked.

"Goodness me, no!" said Mother. "Now it can grow up along with Little Marit, and I'm sure it's going to look after her well."

"That it will." Grandfather nodded. "It'll be both a nursemaid and a shepherdess, and it'll be grand to have a dog to go to the hills with again."

He put Lady down on the floor. She wandered all around, sniffing here and there, and all of a sudden she made a little pool.

"Oh, you poor thing!" cried Grandmother. "We're forgetting you must get out, and we're forgetting to give you food."

She warmed up some milk for it and took out a good knucklebone she had just used for making soup. Torris, meantime, had carried the pup out into the farmyard, and soon Mother followed with milk and bread.

"We can eat outside today in the lovely sunshine," she said, and they went out and sat on the bench by the sunny wall while the pup lay on the grass enjoying the knucklebone that still had plenty of meat on it.

"She's got food sense," said Grandmother, well pleased.

"She's going to be a good dog," said Grandfather. He bent down and patted Lady's back while with his other hand he took the bone out of her little mouth. Lady lay quite still and watched him.

"That's fine," Grandfather said, and gave her the knucklebone back.

"Why did you do that?" Torris asked.

"To accustom her not to growl or bite when her food is taken from her," said Grandfather. "When Little Marit begins to crawl about on the floor, we must be sure we have a nice, patient dog. But we must never beat it. Remember that boys."

Torris and Bard nodded. Not for anything in the whole wide world would they dream of striking the little creature, so Grandfather had nothing to worry about there.

When the pup had eaten, it went across to Grandmother and wagged its tail, as if to thank her for the food. Then it wandered out into the farmyard, sniffed around, and obviously wanted to get to know its new home. It went very carefully, going with its legs crooked and its snout well stretched out before it toward every new thing it encountered. The farmyard was so very big, and you could never be too sure that a dangerous foe did not lie lurking somewhere!

Uh—there against the wall stood a broom with black bristles sticking out in all directions. What sort of horrid creature was that, now? Lady crept up to it on her tummy, leaped back, and crept forward again. And at last she got a scent of the thing and understood it was nothing alive.

"Yap!" she said bravely, and gave the broom a slap so that it fell over. At the same time she took an enormous leap out of the way, just to be on the safe side. But the broom remained just where it was, without moving, and Lady turned tail contemptuously upon it, and sniffed her way off.

Grandfather chuckled. "She's cautious as well as brave."

"That's what Old John thought, too." said Torris happily. Now he was *quite* sure that Lady was a clever and good puppy.

Blakken stood a short distance off nibbling at some tufts of grass. He didn't seem to have noticed the pup yet. He stood with his back to her and swished his tail to chase the flies.

"Now you'll see something," said Grandfather, laughing softly.

Lady padded straight up to the horse. She sniffed her way eagerly forward, step by step—and before Blakken knew what was happening, he had the little creature among his legs.

"Oh-oh!" said Torris in fright, and was about to run and rescue Lady. But Grandfather held him back.

"Take it easy," he said. "A horse never tramples on anything living, especially not on a little one."

And Grandfather was right.

Blakken stood stock still at once. He naturally saw that this was a tiny thing and that he'd have to be very careful with it. He just turned his head slowly and looked at Lady, while she padded about underneath his belly and sniffed at the four long legs, first the forelegs and then the hind legs.

Perhaps Lady did not realize it was a live animal she had come up against. Perhaps she just took the legs to be some tall posts. In any event, she seemed perfectly confident under the big horse. Yet it must have been a special and thrilling smell, for she suddenly got up on two legs and, leaning against one of Blakken's hind legs, she tried to reach his tail.

But it now seemed to Blakken that the little creature had examined him long enough.

He carefully turned around, moving one leg at a time, lowered his big head, and touching Lady with his muzzle, he blew warm breath out through his broad nostrils, and Lady was completely flattened!

"Eeh," she said in terror, and squeezed herself against the ground, while the horse sniffed over her back. It may well be that she thought the huge animal was going to eat her. Torris felt a bit sorry for her, even though he knew she was safe.

"Shall I get her?" he asked.

"No, just let her be," said Father. "It's as well for them to make friends now."

At length Lady seemed to understand that Blakken was not dangerous, even though he was so big. She cautiously raised her head, poked her little snout up toward the horse's muzzle, and at once felt quite secure. She jumped up and began to frisk in and out among the horse's legs in figures of eight, lost her balance and rolled over on the bends, got to her feet again and continued at full speed, around and around.

"Woof, woof!" she barked joyfully. "Look at me. I've just got a big playmate, and I'm not scared of him, woof, woof!"

Blakken merely stood and followed her with his eyes and nickered softly.

But at last the plump little tub was completely exhausted. She waddled back to the doorstep and clambered up into Grandmother's lap, where she fell asleep at once.

Torris sighed with relief.

"You're a kind one, Blakken," he said, and went over and stroked the horse's muzzle. "Now you're friends."

"Yes, horses and dogs always become friends." Grandfather nodded. "It's worse with the cows. But they'll surely get used to her in time."

Torris hoped so. Nothing must happen to Lady, for what would Bogga say then? So, when the cows came in for milking, Bard and he took Lady with them down to the cow barn to let the animals get to know her.

Some of them scowled a little, and one of the cows nearly kicked the milk pail out of Mother's hands. But when Lady had tripped around the barn for a while, most of them seemed to get used to her. Mother thought it would work well in time.

Finally puss arrived, wanting her squirt of milk, as usual, and Lady wandered innocently over to her to play. But when puss arched her back and hissed, Lady knew at once that she should keep clear. She backed away, and puss turned her tail on her and carried on as if she didn't exist.

"Just wait." Grandmother laughed. "Puss will respect Lady a bit more when she grows up, and it won't be long before they'll be the best of friends."

When evening came, it was a tired little pup that lay down to sleep. Grandmother prepared a good bed for her in the corner by the hearth. She took a low basket and laid a bit of old sheepskin in the bottom, along with Gunhild's little doll's blanket. The pup sniffed at her place for a while and then jumped into the basket. Perhaps she recognized the smell of the blanket and felt there was something familiar about it.

She looked about herself once or twice, yelped a bit,

and wanted up on Grandmother's lap. It was as if she felt herself safest with her. So did all the animals on the farm. It was to her they came when something upset them.

But Grandmother took her spinning wheel over to the hearth and put the pup back in the basket again.

"There, there," she said, and patted it. "Now we're just grand. You're missing the warmth of your mother and the other pups, but that'll be all right in a day or two—you'll see. Yes, you'll have forgotten a whole lot by tomorrow, for you're just a little baby. Everything will be fine, just fine." She chatted away as she set the spinning wheel in motion.

The pup listened to Grandmother's voice, and stared at the fire in the hearth and the wheel going around and around. It blinked its eyes once or twice, sighed a little, and curled itself up. And at last it went to sleep.

Then Torris, too, realized how very tired he was and slipped off to bed.

So much had happened that day. It all buzzed around in his head.

There was the journey to the village, the eagle and the Black Gorge, Beret and the keg of flour, Bogga, the minister and the white mare, the pauper child and Gunhild with her braids—and the puppy. And long before little brother Bard had come to bed, he drifted off to sleep with the sound of the spinning wheel and Grandmother's lullaby in his ears:

> "Now that evening softly falls
> it is time for babe to sleep,
> warmly wrapped in skin of sheep
> within a little closet's walls . . ."

Torris was asleep before she had finished the verse.

"Is Torris sick?" asked Bard, alarmed.

"Far from it," said Grandmother with a laugh. "His head's just so full of adventures that there's no room for any more today."

4

Bear Abroad on the Hill

It was a lively company that made its way up to the summer farm the next day.

Out in front raced Torris and Little John, side by side like a pair of lively colts. Then came Old John and John's father with their horse, and lastly came Grandmother and Father with Blakken. Bard, who had also been allowed to come along this time, sat on Blakken's back and shouted with joy, the horses whinnied to each other, and John's little farm dog darted back and forth barking. It was quite sure it had to look after the entire company.

Grandmother had been in some doubt about whether she should stay at home and help Mother. But Mother and Grandfather said that they could easily manage the farm alone for those few days and that Grandmother would be needed to look after all the men on the summer farm. Otherwise, there would be a terrible muddle there. And Grandmother had no objection to a trip to the summer farm in autumn. She had brought two big wooden

pails with her, in case they should come across a cloudberry patch, and there was plenty of good food in the
horse packs.

"Hi, boys, you mustn't run away from us!" Grandmother called.

"We know the way-ay!" Torris called back.

"Mist can co-ome!" yelled Grandmother.

Torris and John laughed till they fell over in the
heather. The sun was blazing over the hills, and the sky
was as blue as a baby's eye.

"Shall we see who gets up to the moor first?" cried
John.

"Yes!" cried Torris, "but we must stick to the track."

And so they set off upward through dwarf birch and
heather-covered rock. There was no risk of running in the
wrong direction. This track to the moor had been trodden
over the years, both by domestic animals and by wild ones.
It wound its way neatly, avoiding all the big stones, just
where it was least trouble to get along. Grandfather had
once said that the animals find the way first, and then men
come along afterward and use their tracks, for it is always
true that animal tracks are the easiest and best.

As Torris pelted off, he thought about who might have
trod the same path before him. Certainly the lynx, on its
way each spring from the valley up to the hill, and possibly
the bear on one of its rare trips down to the village.

He paused for a moment and stared at a huge, solitary
pine, which stood hunched up on its tangled roots. There
could be a bear's den under those roots. But that was nonsense; he had never heard of any such den in these parts,
and it would be rather odd if a bear happened to come
running along here just at this very instant.

He turned and listened. It was all so still. Had John given up? No, there he came at top speed. Torris pelted past the pine, around some huge boulders, and finally up the last steep hill. But then he grew so hot that he had to throw away his smock. He hung it on a bush beside the track and hoped that Father would find it.

At this point John caught up with him, and when he saw Torris without his smock, he took off his. Then they ran on. But they soon grew hot again, and hung up their trousers as well. Two pairs of blue trousers waved on a green branch.

Hey! It was easy to run now. Torris rushed away at John's heels.

But then he noticed that John was quite white from his waist to his knees, and brown above and below, and he began to laugh so much that he couldn't move any more, for it was quite impossible to laugh and run at the same time. And so John was first up.

"I won!" yelled John, and threw out his arms.

"Yes, but you're all white in the middle," gasped Torris, and scrambled up the last stretch.

"So are you!" said John, and roared with laughter. "You look like a winter hare in the middle and a brown bear above and below."

They flopped down upon the heather, gasping with mirth. They were completely exhausted with running and laughing. Now they had to sit and take breath and wait for the others.

But the rest of the company was far behind. They could just hear the dog down the hill. It would be quite some time before they reached them. But that didn't matter at

all, Torris thought, for it was fine to sit here and look out over the valley.

Far below, at the bottom of the valley, lay Bard's Lake, smooth and blue-green, lighter in some parts, darker in others that lay in shadow. From up here one could see how far it extended. It was a fine lake and made the whole valley look more beautiful.

The river was also lovely. It looked like a soft, smooth

band winding its way down among the hills and, as it were, joining mountain, moor, and valley. And from the end of the lake it continued on its way, joining valley and village. From there it flowed for mile after mile, all the way to the sea, perhaps even to the city that Father had spoken of.

The city must be a fine place. Father had been there once, before he married Mother, and he said there was a huge church there, called the Nidaros Cathedral. It was so enormous that all the buildings on the manse farm could be contained inside it. And there were so many houses in the city and so many people that they could not be counted, Father said. What fun it would be to go there once!

Torris slowly turned his head.

His eyes saw a sun-filled moor with white mountain peaks all around, flaring red and purple heather slopes, and a green tarn, which reflected the bobbing tufts of white bog cotton that grew at the edge of the clear water.

It was lovely!

And without knowing clearly why, he suddenly felt beside himself with joy. He wanted to rush along the moor!

"Shall we run to the pool and bathe?" he cried, leaping to his feet.

"Yes!" shouted John.

So they raced along and plunged into the tarn, drank the pure, cool water, ducked under and jumped up. It was cold, but it was not deep, and so there was no danger. When finally they began to feel their skin tingling, they ran ashore and shook themselves. Then they threw themselves down on the warm grass and let the sun dry their bodies.

Torris did not know how long they had been lying sunning themselves when suddenly Grandmother stood there.

"My, if there aren't two boys lying here stark naked!" she cried.

"What else did you expect when we have all their clothes," said Father, who was following. "Shall we have a dip, too, lads?"

"Why not?" replied Ola, John's father.

"Me, too!" cried Bard. He had toiled up the last few slopes and was very hot. They had rarely experienced so warm a September day.

"Please yourselves," grunted Old John, and trudged on without stopping. There would be no bathing for him. As if they wouldn't get enough water on their bodies when they had to wade through the bogs looking for the sheep, he muttered angrily.

"We'll go on ahead, then, boys," said Grandmother. "It isn't far now to the summer farm, and I have new-baked scones in the pack."

Torris and John scrambled into their trousers. They were suddenly very hungry and could hardly wait to get there. Old John was already some little way ahead. They had not gone very far, however, when they noticed that Old John stopped on the path. He had come to a trickle of water and stood there bent over, staring at the ground. He had put the lead on the dog. It yelped and wanted loose, but he held it tightly behind him.

"What's up?" Grandmother called. "Are you going to bathe after all? The water's a bit shallow for that," she joked.

Old John did not answer. He just handed the dog to Little John. Then he bent down and stared at the wet, sandy soil. He stood like that for quite some time, and the others understood this much, that it was a footprint he had caught sight of, but what kind it was they did not know. Nor did they dare to walk up to him and disturb him.

At last Old John straightened himself and looked out over the moor.

"What is it, Granddad?" asked Little John excitedly.

The old man mumbled for a moment inside his beard.

"There's a bear abroad on the hill," he muttered.

Complete silence followed for a time. They weren't sure if they had heard correctly.

Grandmother stood staring at Old John as if she had seen a ghost.

"Do you really think so?" she said in a low voice.

"Look for yourself," replied the old man.

The boys threw themselves down on their knees beside the trickle of water. They held on tightly to the dog between them and stared. Grandmother peered over their shoulders.

At first none of them saw anything except a clear mark of one of Old John's boots. But then Little John saw a faint impression just above it and pointed.

Torris nodded that he, too, had seen it. It was a big footmark, slightly oblong. They could barely manage to make out the marks of the long toes.

But Old John had noticed it, even though he was merely walking along. . . . It was hard to believe. He had eyes like an eagle!

"Don't ruin the marks for me," said the old man.

The boys leaped aside.

"How long is it since the bear has been here?" whispered Grandmother. It sounded as if she were afraid that the bear might come bursting out of the bushes at any moment.

"It was here early today," replied Old John.

"Oh, goodness, then it's not far away," Grandmother whispered. "And our sheep!"

Torris was thinking the same thing.

The sheep—where were they? Little Maid! He had not thought about the lamb since he had been in the village. He had been so taken up with Lady. Now he turned cold with fright and almost believed it was his fault if something had happened to the lamb.

Little Maid, who was so tiny when they let her out in the springtime! She who had danced around him, bleating and wriggling her curly tail. The bear mustn't get her!

But where was she now on the great wide moor?

When he was here earlier with Grandmother at the summer farm, he had seen the flock of sheep several times. Sometimes they were away for many days out of sight; sometimes they came right up to the farm to greet them, and he had seen the lamb growing bigger each time and getting along fine. But she was not big enough to run away from a bear. The fully grown sheep couldn't do so either, for that matter.

Torris looked over at Old John standing there so gruff and silent.

"Where is the bear now, do you think?" he dared to ask.

"Dunno," replied Old John.

"Can you follow the footprints?" asked Little John.

"Hard to," replied Old John. "It's not easy to follow tracks in dry heather—not very far, at least."

"But maybe your dog can?" Grandmother said.

"We'll see," said the old man. He was not the one to let his tongue wag or promise too much.

Finally the others arrived, and Old John showed them the bear prints. "There . . . there . . . and there," he said, and pointed.

The men went down on their knees and looked carefully at the ground. Torris and John stared as well. They had not noticed more than the one footprint that was fairly clear. Old John had discovered two more, although they were so faint that even Father and Ola had difficulty in distinguishing them. Old John saw everything. It was almost uncanny.

"It's a great big fellow," said Father at length, straightening himself up, "a he-bear, I reckon."

"Or an old she-bear," said Ola.

"It has gone in that direction," said Old John, pointing westward.

"How do you know that?" burst out Torris.

"It has trampled down some small twigs here and there," replied the old man.

The boys looked at him in wonderment, and the men talked a little among themselves. They agreed that Ola and Old John should set off with the dog to see whether they could find out where the bear had gone. Father would go on to the summer farm. They couldn't risk letting Grandmother and the youngsters go alone when they had a bear in the neighborhood.

The horses were also restive. They seemed to have gotten a faint scent of wild animal.

Grandmother stood for a moment following the two men with her eyes.

"Well, well"—she sighed—"if it's a good-tempered bear and doesn't harm the sheep, then let it go in peace."

"You're quite right," said Father. "There's no reason to believe the worst. I for my part certainly haven't heard of any killer bear here since I was a boy."

"Maybe it's on the way to its den," suggested Bard.

"No, it's too early in the autumn," Father said. "It has probably just gone looking for some place to sleep for the day. But come along now. I guess we're all pretty hungry."

"As a bear!" said Grandmother, beginning to walk faster.

5

Mountain Wind

They soon reached the summer farm.

It was strange to come there so late in the autumn. The low houses seemed so small and lonely.

No cows came lowing to Grandmother. No calves frolicked in the meadow. The grass had begun to wither and lay in yellow tussocks here and there. It was sad, really.

But when they came into the living room and had a fire going in the hearth, everything seemed more inviting.

Father carried in the horse packs, and Grandmother wasted no time getting the food out and the frying pan over the fire. When the bacon began to sizzle, it at once smelled cozy and homey. They sat down to table and began to eat, and shortly afterward the two bear hunters also arrived.

"Well, how did you get on?" Father asked.

There was not a trace of the bear. The dog had lost the scent fairly soon, and it was impossible to run around in search of broken twigs of heather in the vast moor.

"Quite right," said Grandmother. "Come and eat. The bear is most likely miles away, and you can look for the sheep tomorrow morning."

"We're going today," said Old John.

"Oh, no, surely not," said Grandmother, and stopped with the frying pan in her hand. "You're bound to be tired now, aren't you?"

"We're going today," repeated Old John, chewing so hard that his beard shook.

Father and Ola looked at each other.

It had been a warm journey up and they quite fancied a rest now. They could set out after the sheep in the morning. Neither of them wanted more wandering about in the blazing sun.

But it was not easy to gainsay Old John. Both of them were in the habit of obeying him from their boyhood days. And he was probably right. The sun was still high in the sky, and there were many hours of daylight left.

"Right then. When we've eaten and had a bit of a rest, we might as well get going," Father agreed. "We might take a look in the direction of Blue Cairn."

"The sheep are over by Snota," said Old John. "We'll go there."

Father and Ola looked at each other again.

It was farther to Snota.

But when Old John said that's where the sheep were, he was sure to be right. The old man had a nose like a beagle.

"That's settled, then," Father said. "Thank you for the meal!"

The three men lay down on their bunks, put their jackets over their faces, and fell asleep.

Ola snored with a deep, rumbling noise, Old John

squeaked like a rusty weathercock, and Father pitched in with a flute trill now and then. It sounded like a whole orchestra.

The boys put their hands over their mouths and grinned, but Grandmother hushed them. The men were much in need of their sleep. She quietly cleared the table, and when they awoke half an hour later, they each drank a cup of milk, put food in their packs, and set off over the moor.

"I'm glad I'm not a man," Grandmother said, shaking her head. "I'd never have managed that."

"Yes, you certainly would if you'd been a man!" Torris laughed.

"Oh, you word-splitter, you." Grandmother laughed and flapped him around the ears with the washing-up cloth.

They sat down on the doorstep and watched the men going.

Torris and Little John had been somewhat disappointed about not being allowed to join the search for the sheep. But Grandmother had insisted that they stay home.

"I need some men to look after me when there's a bear roaming about here," she had said. And that was, indeed, perfectly reasonable.

She walked over to the corner of the house, cupped her hands to her mouth, and called out: "Tikka, tikka, tikka, tullan . . . tikka, tikka, tikka, tullan!"

That was the call she always used when she wanted to bring the sheep in. But there was no reply.

"Oh, no—I just hope the menfolk are luckier," she said. "How far have they gone now?"

All four of them shaded their eyes.

Yes, there they were, a good distance over the moor. Old John was out in front, naturally. He loped along at his own steady pace that neither of the others could match. It was unbelievable how quickly he got along on those short bandy legs of his.

He looked like a little gnome, thought Torris. And he seemed to be one with the rocks and the moss. Then he vanished behind a hummock, while Father and Ola were still a good bit behind him, looking like two tall, dark poles against the light moor.

"Some speed Old John has got," Grandmother said.

"Yes, no one can manage to keep up with him," said Little John. "Some say the stones move aside for him, and some say Grandpa gets wings and flies like a bird as soon as he reaches the moors."

"That's just nonsense," said Torris. "No people have wings, and stones can't move."

"No-oh," said John, and was a little put out.

"But I know how he's such a good hunter," said Torris quickly. "It's 'cause he can get in among the animals much more easily when he can walk like that, almost without being seen. I wish I could learn how to do it."

Little John straightened himself.

This grandfather of his was sometimes a bit of a bother for him, but nobody could deny that he was the best huntsman for fifty miles around.

It was as if some of the light fell upon Little John, too, whenever anyone praised the old man.

Now all three men had disappeared, and Grandmother got up.

"I'd better put things in order. Bring in a little water for me, boys," she requested.

The boys each took a bucket and ran to the stream. They carried water until Grandmother was satisfied. Then they sat down on the warm flagstone and wondered what they should do next.

"Pick berries," suggested Bard.

He was so fond of cloudberries.

"Sure, but you've got to remember that the bear may very well be around," said Torris.

Then Bard was not keen on picking berries after all. He would rather stay at home with Grandmother.

"We can all go along together shortly," called Grandmother, who had heard what they were chatting about. "We don't need to go any farther than the nearest patch."

"Can John and I run on in front?" asked Torris.

Grandmother was somewhat doubtful.

But when they promised not to run any farther than she could see them and call to them, they were allowed to chance it. She gave them pails for picking in, and they slipped out of the door.

It did not take them more than a few minutes to run to the patch. There the cloudberries grew in thick clusters, plump, golden, and juicy. At least the bear had not been here, for then there wouldn't have been a single one left. It was well known that he was fond of sweet berries.

The boys first ate as much as they could. Then they picked enough to cover the bottom of the pails, or so. But they soon tired of it. They could wait till Grandmother arrived, suggested Torris, for then the picking would go much faster.

John agreed.

"Shall we hurry on to the top of that hill there?" he said, pointing. "We may be able to see some sheep from there."

Torris turned his head this way and then that, measuring the distance from the houses to the top of the hump.

Yes, it should be all right. From the top they could easily see down to the summer farm, and it was no farther than they could hear Grandmother, should she call.

"Right, come on!" he cried. "We'll leave the pails here."

They jumped through the clumps of heather and soon stood on the low hump where they had a view across the whole moor. They threw themselves down on their stomachs on the heather and gazed all around.

How grand it was!

On all sides were gleams of light from little tarns and mountain streams. Here and there were summer farms huddling between the hillocks. They caught sight of John's farm, too, even though the turf roof almost merged with the hillside. And all around the vast moor lay the mountains, ridge after ridge of them.

The boys vied with each other as to who could remember most of their names. There was Blue Top and Noon Top, Okla and Snota, Double Hat and Bun Top and Long Ridge. And there were more and still more, peak upon peak. They did not remember them all, but John knew most.

"Oh, but look over there!" he cried, and pointed to the foot of Blue Top. "There is something moving. I wonder —could it be the sheep?"

Torris looked around quickly.

Yes, there was something. It was a big herd of animals. He saw it moving, spreading out like a huge fan, moving back and forth in waves.

"It's reindeer," he said, for he knew the way they moved.

Sheep moved differently. They were much slower and often went singly or in pairs, so that they appeared as small, scattered specks of white.

"There are many animals in that herd," he said. Probably many calves, too. If only the bear isn't over there now."

"Oh! I hope not!" said John.

But then something else caught Torris's eye.

He had happened to glance skyward to see the position of the sun, and at that very moment his gaze met a large bird sweeping around and around in a wide circle over their heads.

"Look!" he cried. "That's an eagle! What do you think it's got its eye on?"

"Couldn't be us, could it?" asked John doubtfully.

"No-oh, an eagle won't attack boys as big as us, certainly not when there are two of us. But there must be something it's looking at."

They lay down on their backs and kept an eye on it. It would be fun to see if it dived. Perhaps it was watching lemmings or other little creatures. Torris had never seen an eagle dive, but Father had told him that it clapped its mighty wings together and shot like an arrow toward the ground.

It must be exciting to watch.

They followed the eagle with their eyes as it sailed up there in the blue heavens—around and around and around. They grew quite dizzy with this and began to laugh.

But in the midst of their laughter Torris heard a sound.

"Hush!" he said and half sat up.

"Uh?" said John.

"Didn't you hear?" whispered Torris.

"No, hear what?" asked John, and sat up as well.

They both stared around and listened, but all was still.

"How queer," Torris said. "There was something, quite close."

"Maybe just a bird," suggested John. "Or perhaps your grandma?"

They stared toward the summer farm, but there was no-body to be seen there.

Then all at once it came again—clearly.

It went "Ehhh!"

Oh, help! The boys jumped up and stared, without mov-ing, at the place the sound came from. They were ready to pelt away in a flash. But they didn't know if they dared do *that* either. Torris's heart was beating right up in his throat. Surely it could never be . . . ?

Then suddenly he saw it.

Just below the hump, on the side away from the summer farm, there were some huge boulders, and half hidden be-hind them something was moving. At first he saw only a light back, then a head sticking up, and lastly a pair of frightened eyes staring at them.

Torris stared back and slowly breathed out.

It was only a reindeer calf, a poor little frightened and helpless creature, which stood looking around in a panic.

John saw it at the same moment.

"Gosh, it's a reindeer calf!" he cried. "It's stuck."

They ran down the slope.

When they came closer, the calf grew frightened. It

thrust this way and that, struggling to free itself. But there was something gripping it by one of its hind legs.

Torris went carefully up to it.

"There, now," he said softly, just as Grandmother was in the habit of saying to quiet animals, "they-eyre, now . . ."

The calf threw up its head.

"Ehhh!" it said once more.

It was a queer, hoarse lowing, light and frightened. Maybe it was trying to call to its mother, but she was far away by now. She was almost certainly with the big herd over at Blue Top, for this was the law of the wild reindeer. The herd was continually on the move, and if a calf could not keep up with it, the mother just had to leave it.

Torris stretched out his hand. He laid it on the neck of the little creature and stroked its coat.

Oh, how fine it was—light and lovely from its head down its back, and darker, on its flanks. Its eyes were large and shiny, and the fur on its forehead was curly.

But it looked tired and weak. How long might it have been stuck there? For a day, perhaps—or maybe two?

Torris sat down on his haunches and went on stroking the calf as he chatted to it. And at length it seemed to grow calmer.

John had remained a short distance away. He knew it was better that they shouldn't both come barging along together. Such things he had learned from his grandfather. But when he saw that the calf was quieting down, he slithered down to Torris.

"The eagle is still flying up there," he said. "It's certainly the calf it has been watching. We'll have to get it loose."

Torris looked up.

Yes, there it was, the huge bird of prey. It was bound to get angry now, for it must have been waiting for the calf to die so that it could get a good meal for itself. If only it didn't start diving down on them to try to scare them off. It could be dangerous if those enormous wings began flapping about their ears. Father had said there was as much power in the blow from an eagle's wing as in a horse's kick.

But the eagle remained up there, fortunately, and the boys began to investigate how they could get the reindeer calf free.

There was a small cleft between two stones where the calf was standing.

The little creature had probably been trying to get at some reindeer moss at the foot of the cleft, but then a flat stone had toppled over and clamped one of its hind legs tightly. Perhaps the stone had turned over when the calf had brushed against it. If they were to free the animal, they must, at any rate, get the stone out of the way.

"I'll get a hold of it," John said. "I think I can manage."

He sat down behind the calf with his back arched against one of the boulders, took hold of the flat stone with both hands, and prized it upward.

It moved slightly.

John held on. He was quite red in the face. "Get a hold and pull from the other side!" he yelled.

Torris lay on his stomach over a boulder on the other side of the cleft. He tightened his grasp around the stone and pulled for all he was worth, while John pushed.

They managed to tilt it on one edge. But if they let go, it would fall down on the calf once more.

"I'll hold on while you pull out the calf," shouted Torris.

John let go.

"Hurry!" gasped Torris. He had to hold tight with all his strength.

John wasted no time about throwing his arms around the little creature and pulling it out. The calf was frightened and struggled against him, but John lifted it up by its hind quarters and heaved, and at last it was free.

Torris let go of the stone. It fell down again with a crash, and the boys sank down, breathless, in the heather beside the calf.

There it lay.

Once or twice it put its forelegs under it and tried to rise, but it could not manage—merely toppled over and lowed. It certainly was both weak and hungry, and its leg must also be hurting.

"We must try to carry it along to the farm," said Torris.

"Yes," said John. "We must go around the hump. That's the easiest."

The calf lay openmouthed, staring at them. It was frightened, but that couldn't be helped, for it couldn't remain lying there. They both took hold of it, Torris around its chest and John around its hindquarters, and at length they managed to lift it up.

But the calf was bigger than they had supposed. The four long, thin legs straggled down to the ground, and when they had walked a short distance, they realized that it was pretty heavy as well. Besides, the ground was very rough here.

"I wish Grandma would come soon," panted Torris when they were halfway around the hump.

"Maybe she's at the berry patch now," said John. "If we go a little bit farther, we'll see it."

"Let's have a rest first," said Torris.

They laid the calf on the grass and sat down beside it. A tiny brook trickled by. It was peaty water and not very good, but the calf was thirsty, for it turned its head and looked at the water, and when they eased it closer, it put its muzzle down and drank.

Torris looked up for the eagle.

No, it had gone. It had given up when it saw them carrying the calf away. A good thing they had found it—before it was too late.

"Who's that coming along over there?" John asked suddenly.

"Where?" asked Torris, for he didn't see anybody.

"Over by the tarn," said John, pointing. "Surely the men can't be coming from that direction?"

Torris couldn't see anyone. Yes, there, far away, something was moving. But it wasn't people. It was an animal. Could it be Old John's dog?

"I don't understand," he said. "It's an animal, but it isn't running like a dog."

"No-oh," said John. "But what is it then? It's not a reindeer either."

They both stared at it. It was still too far away for them to see properly, and then it disappeared behind a knoll.

"Maybe it was a wolverine?" said John.

"Or a lynx," said Torris.

They sat waiting and stared toward the knoll. Where on earth had the animal gone?

Then John suddenly got to his feet.

"There—th-there it is!" he stammered.

Torris saw it the selfsame moment. It had appeared on the right side of the knoll and was much closer than they had thought. It was big and dark brown in color, with a thick coat. It lumbered along at a steady pace, heading straight for them.

It was the bear!

Torris and John both stiffened. For a moment it was as if they couldn't do a thing. Then they started running.

But all of a sudden they stopped.

The calf!

They rushed back without a word, picked up the calf between them, and ran as quickly as they could by the straightest route, struggling upward step by step, scratching their legs on the tough heather stalks, but caring nothing for that—just upward, until they could see the summer farm.

Grandmother must be in the berry patch, Torris prayed. She *had* to be there!

He cast a glance behind him. The bear was coming! He thought it was much closer now. He could see its head quite clearly, and the broad paws that plodded forward through the heather. It was huge.

"Hurry!" he gasped to John, who was going in front.

But it was not so easy to move forward quickly with the calf between them. Torris thought the heather was twice as high as it had been and the way up to the top twice as long as the way down. Suppose the bear caught up with them? Then they would have to abandon the calf.

No, they *mustn't* do that. They had to manage!

And then, at last, they heard a voice calling to them from quite close. They didn't take time to reply, just ran. A moment later they were on top of the little hill, and they almost tumbled right into the arms of Grandmother, who had come up from the other side with Bard.

"Gracious me!" said Grandmother, looking from the boys to the calf. "What's going on?"

"The bear!" gasped Torris. "It's right behind us. We've got to run."

Grandmother gave a start.

Then she stood quite calmly.

"Where's the bear?" she asked.

"There!" said Torris and John, turning to point.

But where? What had become of it? They stood there, in astonishment, staring all around, but were so flustered that they did not know where to look.

Grandmother laughed softly.

"That's right, so it is," she said, and pointed. "It's the bear and no mistake, but I don't think we'll need to run."

The boys looked, and over where Grandmother was pointing, they caught sight of it. It lay on its back on a little grassy slope playing with itself, its four paws in the air. It was much farther away than they had supposed, and it didn't look half as frightening as before.

"It—it's playing!" Torris gasped. He could not believe his own eyes.

"Yes, indeed, it's playing," said Grandmother with a smile. "It doesn't look so dangerous now, does it?"

"No," said John, drawing a deep breath. "I didn't know that bears played."

"Oh, yes, they do," Grandmother said. "Even wild animals play when they are in a good mood."

"Do you think it's seen us?" Torris asked. He was still not wholly convinced that the bear wouldn't come racing after them with open jaws.

"No, it hasn't seen us," said Grandmother. "Bears are shortsighted, and the wind is blowing from it to us, so it hasn't caught our scent either. But perhaps it knows about our cloudberry patch."

"Then it'll come here," said John.

"Yes, it's very likely, so we'll go down to the farm now," said Grandmother. "But when I see the bear like this, I'm much less afraid of him than when I just see his tracks." She laughed.

They took another look at the huge beast as it lay there enjoying itself on the sunny green hillside. Then Grandmother put her arms around the reindeer calf and helped to carry it. She didn't ask anything about it, and the boys didn't say anything either. That could wait till they were home.

"Was that the bear?" asked Bard as he trotted along beside Grandmother.

"It was the bear, yes," said Grandmother. "Wasn't it funny?"

"Yes," said Bard. "It lay on its back and rolled just like Blakken when he goes out to grass."

Torris and John looked at each other. Bard was four years old and afraid of nothing.

But Torris remembered when he himself was four years old and feared nothing—before he knew that anything could be dangerous.

They reached the summer farm, and the boys and Grandmother carried the reindeer calf right into the summer cow barn, where they laid it down on some dry hay. Grandmother brought fresh water for it, and then they told her the whole story.

"It was fine you found it," Grandmother said. "It's a beautiful calf, and I don't think it's so badly hurt that we can't get it well again. Father will have to take a look at the leg when he comes home."

She went out and soon came back in again with a little reindeer moss, which she placed in front of it. When the calf recognized the fresh smell of the moss, it poked out its muzzle and nibbled at it.

"There we are," Grandmother said, and stroked its neck. "So long as you have your food sense, there's hope for you. Now we'll leave you in peace, and then perhaps you'll recover. By the way," she added, "we'll bring the horses in to you as well, so that you'll have a little company."

She went out and called in the two horses, and let them into the summer cow barn, where they made straight for the little creature and sniffed it. But the calf did not seem to be afraid. It lay quite at ease. And when Grandmother had watched it for a while, she went out with the boys and saw that the door was securely bolted.

"That's that," she said. "Now we'll go in and have some supper."

It was still clear daylight, but the sun was rapidly sinking, and the air was growing chill. The boys ran to the stream and fetched more water, and when they returned, Grandmother had placed a huge log on the hearth and hung the porridge pot over the fire.

"Autumn is coming," she chatted. "It'll be early dark. I hope the men manage to get back before night."

"But there's a moon, Grandma," said Torris, "almost a full moon."

"Yes, that's a fact," said Grandmother. "I'm beginning to grow old and forgetful. No, there's no danger, then. The sky's so clear now that it'll be a fine, bright night. But it'll be exciting to see if they come home with the sheep."

She walked about, laying the table, stirring the porridge, and now and then casting a glance out of the little window. Suddenly she clapped her hands together.

"Oh, how stupid of us—we've left our cloudberry pails out at the berry patch," she said.

"We can run and fetch them," suggested John.

"No-oh, there's no hurry before the morning," Grandmother said. "It's too late to pick berries now, anyway."

"But it's still light," said Torris.

"It can wait till tomorrow," repeated Grandmother.

Torris looked at her in surprise. It surely wasn't like Grandmother to put anything off till tomorrow. And what about the fine cloudberry pails that Grandfather had made last winter? No, there was something odd—something quite unusual about Grandmother this evening.

Could it have something to do with the bear?

She had also taken in the horses. Blakken usually stayed out in the field all night as long as there was good weather. Was it really for the sake of the calf that she had brought the horses in, as she had said? And then that constant looking out of the window! Now she went out to the woodshed as well and gazed out through the Dutch door. She kept finding excuses for going out there to look out over the moor.

Yes, Grandmother was expecting something.

And suddenly there it was, whatever Grandmother had been expecting.

She had just taken another quick turn out to the shed and came back at once.

"Come and see, boys," she said, and beckoned to them. "We've got a guest in our berry patch."

John and Bard looked at her in amazement. But Torris rushed out and hitched himself onto the Dutch door.

There it was, the bear, just a few stones' throws away. It lumbered around, snuffling and eating cloudberries till the juice streamed down its jaws, using its paws to shovel them in, and was quite beside itself with delight over its delicious evening meal.

Torris very nearly laughed out loud, and John and Bard hung across the door with eyes as round as saucers.

"The bear!" whispered Bard.

"Your cloudberry pails!" said John.

"He's eating up all the good berries," said Bard, looking angrily at the bear.

"We'll just have to let him," said Grandmother with a chuckle. "So long as he's a nice bear, he may eat as much as he can manage."

Just then the bear spotted the two pails. He padded up to them, sniffed suspiciously at one of them, and gave it such a thump that it flew through the air. The cloudberries rolled out in all directions, and the bear wasted no time in guzzling them. Then he went over to the empty pail and sniffed in it.

"Brrrh!" he said scornfully, and thumped it again.

But he treated the second pail more properly. The bear understood now that the strange things contained something good. He took the pail between his forepaws and stuck his whole head inside—and yum, yum, there he stood eating like a baby, rocking his body and grunting

and smacking his lips so that he could be heard a long way off.

"See how he's enjoying himself," whispered Grandmother.

"How huge he is," whispered John.

"Yes, he's no little 'un," said Grandmother.

"What if he sees us?" asked Torris.

"He neither sees us nor smells us. Besides, he thinks the summer farm's empty," replied Grandmother. "He has probably been going about keeping his eye on this berry patch since we went down with the cattle, and now he's come to gather the berries. I was pretty sure we'd see him here this evening."

"Was that why you took in the horses, Grandma?" Torris asked.

"Yes, that was exactly why," Grandmother said. "Horses go crazy when they get the scent of a bear, so I was afraid they'd bolt away across the moor."

The bear had now emptied the other pail as well. He was still holding it between his paws, and when he did not find any more, threw it away with a grunt and sat down, looking around him. His big paws hung down across his belly, and he looked for all the world like a good dog "begging nicely." Then he scratched his chest a little, arose, and began to search for more berries.

"Is he allowed to eat up *all* the berries?" asked Bard, looking angrily at the bear.

"Hush, you mustn't talk so loudly, or he'll hear us," whispered Grandmother.

But Bard paid no attention to her.

"You're not allowed to eat them all up!" he yelled.

The bear stopped abruptly. He reared up to his full height on his hind legs and glared toward the farmhouse, waving his paws about and turning his head this way and that, growling.

Grandmother, Torris, and John held their breaths. But Bard seemed to think he was now on speaking terms with the bear.

"No, because I want some berries, too," he yelled. "It's our berry patch, you see!"

Torris threw himself at Bard and placed his hand firmly over his mouth.

"Be quiet!" he whispered.

"Oh, mercy me!" said Grandmother, going backward.

"Has he seen us?" whispered John.

"No, he's too shortsighted for that. But he heard Bard, that's quite certain," said Grandmother. "I wonder what he's going to do now?"

They all stared anxiously at the bear. Even Bard was still. He realized at last that this was no game.

The bear stood there snorting and trying to get the scent of what he had heard. He was familiar with human voices and knew they had something to do with the summer farm buildings. But it must have been a surprise to him that there were people now, and he was very curious. He lumbered forward a few paces. Then he went down on all fours and came slowly nearer.

"What shall we do if he comes here?" Torris whispered.

"Then we'll have to bolt the door," whispered Grandmother, shoving the boys away from the door.

"But if he tries to bash in the door?"

"Then I'll have to take the old gun and shoot out the window," said Grandmother. Her voice quavered slightly.

"Can you shoot, Grandma?" asked Torris.

"No—oh yes, if I shut my eyes so I don't have to see the horrible gun, then I'll sure enough dare to fire it."

Torris looked at her and couldn't help smiling.

If it had been Bogga, she'd have shot like a general, if need be. But Grandmother! Her aim would certainly be poor if she was going to shoot in the way she said.

"Do you really think you could hit it that way, Grandma?" he asked.

"Are you crazy, boy!" said Grandmother, horrified. "I

had no intention of shooting at the bear. No, I'll just shoot up in the air and give him a bit of a fright."

The bear had now reached the end of the berry patch. There he remained standing with his head thrust out, giving low growls from the depths of his broad chest. He didn't like not being able to smell what he had heard.

Perhaps he could just see something moving in the doorway. But he'd have to go around to the other side of the farm to have the wind blowing from the right direction so that he could get a proper scent. He set off that way and vanished behind a knoll.

Grandmother had seen so many bears in her time that she guessed what he would do now.

"Come," she said. "Unless I'm mistaken, we'll see him on the other side of the farm."

They all ran right through the woodshed and peeped out through the door to the south. They stood there quite some time and had almost given up when John sighted something moving.

It was the bear right enough.

He had run in a wide arc around the farm, and now he stood on a little hill some distance off, sniffing and slowly nodding his great head. His eyes blinked, small and short-sighted, toward the buildings. But he now caught the smell of smoke from a chimney, people and animals, and knew what he was dealing with. His sensitive nose told him that, now that the wind was coming from the proper quarter.

"No, this is no place for me," he was probably thinking. "Better get out of here."

And so the bear lumbered off, padding smoothly along between the hillocks, and vanished into the blue dusk.

Grandmother sighed.

"Very well," she said, relieved. "So I didn't have to shoot. That's just what I thought—it was a good bear."

"But it certainly was exciting," John said.

Grandmother stared in the direction in which the great beast had disappeared.

"Wonder what your Grandad will say when he hears about this?" She chuckled.

"Oho!" said John, his eyes round as marbles. "Bet he'll be mad because he wasn't here."

It grew dark, and they ate their supper.

Afterward they took a walk down to the cow barn and had a look at the reindeer calf. It lay asleep in the hay, but when Grandmother held the lantern above it, it raised its head and blinked sleepily from under its long eyelashes.

"Yes, you are really beautiful," said Grandmother. "It looks as though you're also beginning to get used to us."

The horses stood quite still, sleeping.

Grandmother patted their necks, and then they all went out and shut the door.

As soon as they returned, they crept into their bunks.

There was soft new hay in them, smelling good and fresh. Torris and John jumped up into either end of one bunk. Bard was to sleep with Grandmother.

"You'll have to try to get a little sleep, boys," she said as she went to sit beside the hearth with her knitting. "It'll be a long day tomorrow, too."

Torris closed his eyes.

But he couldn't manage to fall asleep. He was too excited and wondered whether the men would have the sheep with them when they returned, and Little Maid!

"Do you think it will be long before they come, Grandma?" he asked, sitting up.

"It's impossible to say," replied Grandmother. "Maybe they'll come soon, maybe not till near morning. Depends how far they've got to go."

Torris lay down again. He looked at the fire glow flickering over walls and roof. Light and shade came and went over the beams, and his eyes grew heavy with watching it.

"Is it moonlight outside now?" he asked.

"It hasn't risen yet," Grandmother said. "But it will be up soon."

Torris thought he saw the moors before him in the moonlight. The mists of night swirled across them, and now and then an animal rustled softly in the heather. A little weasel awoke and crawled out of its hole. It sniffed out at the night and stared with its beady black eyes at the face of the moon. Then it scuttled off over the heathery ridges. And there the bear, big and heavy, lumbered along. He was sleepy and wanted to get to his den and sleep.

But suddenly he stopped.

Right in front of him stood a white lamb bleating, alone and deserted on the wide moor.

"What are you doing all by yourself up here on the hill?" growled the bear.

"I'm lost," bleated the lamb. "I can't find my mother."

"That's a shame," said the bear. "You should have stayed with the flock."

"Yes, but I was playing," said the lamb, "and then I lost sight of the others."

"What's your name, then?" asked the bear.

"Little Maid, Bard's Farm," replied the lamb.

"Oh, I see. Then you belong down there at the summer

farm where I was today," said the bear. "I'll see you home, though I'm very sleepy. Come on!"

The bear shambled along in front, and the lamb tripped after him with its bell ringing. Torris heard it clearly outside.

"Little Maid!" he shouted, and wanted to run toward it, but there he was suddenly—flat on the floor with the blanket over his head.

"What are you up to, Torris!" cried Grandmother in fright. "You scared the wits out of me."

Torris peered out from beneath the blanket and looked all around in confusion. Bard and John sat upright in their bunks, gazing sleepily at him.

"I thought I heard Little Maid's bell," he said meekly.

"Well, you didn't think so stupidly at that," Grandmother said with a laugh, "even if your lamb has never had a bell on it. But I just heard something myself. Hush!"

There came a sound of many bells from the darkness outside, and bleating and barking and deep voices. Torris sprang up and raced out after Grandmother.

"Father!" he cried. "Have you found Little Maid?"

"Yes, she's here somewhere," shouted Father.

And there were all the sheep streaming into the meadow in the moonlight. Torris ran into the midst of the big flock, was bumped here and there by soft bodies, dug with his fingers into warm, dry wool, and struggled on.

But it was not easy to find Little Maid in all that confusion.

There was bleating in light and deep tones, there was tripping and dancing on all sides, and not one sheep stood still a single instant.

"Little Maid!" he wheedled. "Where are you, Little Maid?"

"Ba-a-a-a!" came from a little distance off.

There Torris's eye fell on a bell-sheep with two lambs, one large and one smaller. Could the little one be Little Maid?

He scrambled over the backs of one or two sheep that stood in his way and reached the lamb. He bent down and looked at its tail.

Yes! It had a brown spot. It was his lamb!

"My Little Maid," he said happily, and squatted down with his arms around her neck.

"Ba-a-a-a-a!" answered the lamb. She poked out her wet mouth and nibbled rapidly and eagerly at Torris's cheek, while she very nearly flattened the toes on his naked feet with her hoofs.

"I think Little Maid recognizes me, Grandma," he shouted, overjoyed.

"Of course she does," said Grandmother, who was sitting on the doorstep with the barn lantern beside her. "You were the one who looked after her when she was little. Just look at these over here and see if they don't recognize me, too."

Yes, it was obvious that the sheep recognized Grandmother. They flocked around her, bleating and jostling to come closest. And when she brought a pinch of salt for them, their excitement knew no bounds. They almost pushed her over, as well as the lantern, and Bard and John had to scurry in through the door.

"There, there, take it easy." She laughed, warding them off.

The men were trying to count the sheep at the other end of the meadow.

"How many animals have you up there?" called Father.

"I've got six ewes here and ten lambs," Grandmother shouted back. "They're all ours. And how big is the minister's flock?"

"There should be exactly forty," said Father. "I think we've got them all."

"Then both the minister and we have been lucky this year, the Lord be praised," said Grandmother, for it often happened that some sheep or other was lost on the hill, having either fallen over a cliff or been killed by wild animals.

Torris was still sitting in his shirt out in the moonlight, hugging Little Maid, while the men and the dog drove the minister's animals into the fold. He felt a bit cold, but that didn't matter. He poked his fingers into the lamb's fleece and rested his chest on its curly back. That soon warmed him up.

Now only their own sheep were left. But they would not leave Grandmother. She had to go in front of them herself and call them after her.

"Tikka, tikka, tikka, come on then, you poo-oo-or little things," she called. And then they came after her at once, butted against her apron, and played up to her.

Little Maid tore herself away from Torris and ran bleating after her mother. But that was as it should be. He couldn't have the lamb inside the house like another puppy dog.

Then they closed the fold and ran in to the warm hearth. Grandmother had food ready for the men and the dog. The boys were allowed to sit on the floor, each wrapped up in a sheepskin, and listen to the story of the search.

They sat there full to bursting with their own secrets. But they had promised Grandmother not to say anything before she gave a sign, and so they sat listening to Father.

"No, there's not really very much to tell," Father said. The sheep had been over by Snota, as Old John had said. He was also the one who had found them, of course, on their way down to another valley. It had been a long trek. But the three men were pleased that they had had such fine weather and found all the animals safe and sound.

Grandmother nodded, and there was silence for a while. Then she glanced over at Old John.

"Did you see anything of the bear, then, you folks?" she suddenly asked.

"Not a whiff of it," replied Old John dourly.

"No-oh, that was hardly to be expected, either . . ." said Grandmother, rocking back and forth on her chair.

The boys glanced up at her and had to hold their hands in front of their mouths to keep themselves from laughing out loud. But the men now became curious. They probably guessed from her tone of voice that she knew something. Old John looked sharply at her from beneath his bushy eyebrows.

"What do you mean by this talk?" he asked. "Have *you* seen it, by any chance?"

"Oh, yes, of course," said Grandmother casually, as if she were talking about a kitten. "We had the bear here nearly half the day. A huge hulk of a bear, as big as a fully grown cow."

At that Old John nearly leaped up to the ceiling.

"Where?" he shouted. "When?"

Father and Ola asked with one voice, "Where . . . when?"

"Just out on the berry patch here," Grandmother said. "Three or four stones' throws away."

"He ate all our cloudberries!" yelled Bard.

"It's quite true!" shouted Torris and John.

"Yes," said Grandmother, chuckling, "we almost thought he'd take a trip into the house."

Old John was completely dumb.

But then the boys, talking all at the same time, told about everything that had happened to them: about the reindeer calf and the bear and the cloudberry patch, and how Grandmother meant to shoot with the gun if the bear came too close.

"You!" snorted Old John, and glared at Grandmother. "Huh! But I can tell you, if only I'd been here . . ."

Grandmother shook her fist at him.

"Old John," she said, "it was a good bear."

"Uh!" grunted Old John. "A bear is a bear."

No, Old John would certainly never get over this.

Torris watched him and was very glad the old huntsman had not been at home. But then he remembered the reindeer calf.

"Can we go down now and take a look at the calf, Father?" he asked.

"No, I'll go and have a look on my own," said Father. "You're for your beds now—we all are."

And there was nothing else for it. It was midnight, and they'd have to be up with the sun. Grandmother raked ashes over the embers in the hearth, and soon they were all asleep, both humans and animals.

But far out on the moor the big bear roamed, well filled

with food, and peered up at the moon with his small, shortsighted eyes.

When Torris awoke next morning, Father had already looked at the reindeer calf.

There was nothing seriously wrong with it. The flat stone had just caught its thigh, which was tender and swollen, making it difficult for it to stand on its leg. But it would certainly get well again, he thought.

"You'll see that in a few months' time it'll run as fast as the mountain wind."

"Oho!" shouted Torris. Now he knew what the calf would be called. It would be called Mountain Wind! And just imagine when it was big enough to pull a sled—then he'd skim along at top speed.

But a thought struck him.

John had been with him when they found the calf, of course, and had just as much right to it. He said so to him.

"Not at all," said John. "It's your calf. You saw it first. And we've no room for it, anyway."

Torris looked at John's father.

"That's quite right, Torris," said Ola. "We've hardly any room for this calf, and John would like you to have it."

"Yes," said John.

And then Torris understood that he meant it.

It was a big crowd that set off homeward.

Grandmother went first, calling the sheep. The big bell-sheep walked next to her. It was quite obvious that they should walk ahead of the flock. The sheep fixed this up among themselves according to rank and years, without having to be told about it by anyone. The lambs tripped along beside their mothers.

John and Torris ran on each side of the track and saw that none of them wandered too far away. And if a sheep forgot itself and stood there eating or a lamb began to leap sideways, then the dog was there at once and chased the sinner back into place.

Last of all came the men with the horses. Bard sat on Blakken's back, and Father walked beside the horse with the reindeer calf across his shoulders.

"Is it heavy, Father?" shouted Torris.

"No, it's so small and thin," said Father. "It weighs almost nothing."

They rested once on the way, and Grandmother found a cloudberry patch beside the track where the bear hadn't been, for there were berries enough to fill the pails.

The reindeer calf was allowed to get down on the ground, meanwhile, and move about a little.

It limped around on three legs, nibbled moss and drank water, and no longer jerked away when they went up to it. It would certainly be tame soon, said Father.

"Do you think Mother and Granddad will be pleased when they see Mountain Wind?" asked Bard.

"Yes, surely," Father said. "For now we'll have two animals to pull the sleds when we go down to the village next year."

"That'll be grand!" said Torris.

He saw in his mind's eye a strong and proud Mountain Wind with big horns and a bell and many-colored harness. He would begin to train it as soon as possible.

But a short time after, when he walked along behind Father and saw the little creature hanging over his neck, with four dangling legs that seemed far too long and thin, he realized that it would indeed be some time before Mountain Wind and he had got *that* far.

6

Lady and Her Friend
from the Wood

The fine autumn weather continued, and that was a good thing. First of all, there was Little Marit's christening down in the village. It was important to have good weather then, for Mother had to sit on Blakken with Little Marit in her arms.

The whole day had been fine in every way, and Torris had been into the manse to greet Bogga and had seen Gunhild's playhouse. Inside it was just like a real little living room, with small tables and chairs and, in addition, a little cupboard with tiny mugs and bowls. He would ask Grandfather to make one like it for Little Marit when she was big enough to play in it.

Torris was also grateful for the good weather for Mountain Wind's sake. As long as the fields were bare and firm, the reindeer calf could go freely about and exercise its leg. It was getting better every day and scarcely limped at all. And when Torris didn't have any jobs to do, Bard and he

played around in the farmyard and wood with Mountain
Wind and Lady.

The puppy grew before their very eyes. She was no
longer so barrel-shaped. She began to have longer legs and
a smoother coat. She had a fine bushy tail lying in a curl
upon her straight back, and she was so willing and clever at
learning things that it was a joy.

When Mother laid Little Marit on the floor to let her
wriggle and stretch herself, Lady lay down nicely beside
her and watched. And if Little Marit lay in her cradle and
started to cry, then the puppy was there at once, getting
up on its hind legs and looking in, as if to see what was the
matter.

Yes, Lady was going to be a good watchdog certainly,
and a clever nursemaid for Little Marit just as Grandfather had said.

But so far Lady was mainly just an inquisitive pup.

Every day she hit on a new and exciting game or discovered something that had to be investigated. And one evening at milking time Torris could not find her anywhere.

What could she have thought up now?

He asked the others, but none of them knew where she
was, and none of them could remember when they had
seen her last. They all had their own business to attend to,
and Lady scurried about here and there as she pleased.

"But wait a moment," Father said, thinking hard.
"When I was busy plowing with the bull this afternoon,
she was running about his legs all the time, and I had to
chase her away."

Torris laughed.

Lady could not make proper friends with the big bull,
however good-tempered and patient he was. She had got-

ten used to the cows, and they had got used to her, too. But it was different with the big bull. It was probably his gruff bellowing that frightened her, and his huge bulk. She always ran yapping around his feet when he was out.

But where was she now?

Torris ran out into the farmyard and shouted in all directions.

No, there was no reply from Lady.

He searched in the barn and in the cow barn, in the stable, and over at the sheep. She was in none of these places. He peered, just to make sure, down into the well, but fortunately she was not there. The little door to the well shed was securely closed, as it should be.

Torris went down to the cow barn again and was quite at a loss.

Lady always used to come when they drove the cows back in the evening. She had discovered that the big animals moved faster when she ran barking at their heels, and she never missed this enjoyable game.

"She'll be here soon enough, you'll see," Mother said. "You must remember she's beginning to grow up, and perhaps she wants to go for trips on her own. Maybe she's up in the wood."

"Yes," said Torris, lifting the broom. He began to muck out the cow barn and thought over what Mother had said.

It was not at all unlikely that Lady was in the wood.

Recently he had seen her coming out of the wood several times, and he had been afraid that she might wander too far away one day or encounter a wild animal. Hitherto she had always come back, but . . .

He finished his mucking-out in haste and went out.

It was beginning to grow dark. He walked here and

there about the meadow, calling, but got no answer. He remained standing, uncertain about what exactly he should do. Then he went back and sat on a millstone that lay near the house.

He would have to wait until Father was finished with his work and ask him to join in the search for the puppy.

Torris did not know for sure which he noticed first, the barking or the stir over there at the edge of the wood. But he suddenly saw Lady coming at full tilt out of the undergrowth.

He was so happy that he jumped up and was just on the point of shouting to her when he saw another animal fast on her heels.

The cry stuck in his throat.

He saw that the animal was right behind Lady and could attack her at any moment. He felt his heart thumping, and he was just about to rush over the meadow when he suddenly realized what kind of animal it was.

It was a fox cub!

It was a quite ordinary little fox cub, of the same size as Lady, lovely and neat, with a reddish yellow coat and a long white-tipped, bushy tail. And it was certainly not going to pounce on Lady. The two puppies were just playing with each other.

Torris sank back on the millstone again.

His knees were wobbly, and his heart was still pounding. He had not had such a fright since he saw the bear.

Swish, the creatures went racing after each other, tumbling over, biting each other's tail, leaping up again and dashing off.

But the whole thing was just fun.

Father knew it, too. He had come up very quietly and now sat down on the stone beside Torris, smiling.

"Lady has found a playmate, I see," he whispered.

"Yes, aren't they funny, Father?" whispered Torris. "I think they've known each other some time."

"Looks like it," said Father. "That must be the reason why Lady's been so much up in the woods recently."

The game continued over at the edge of the wood. They followed each other in and out among the trees, around the foot of pine trees and young birches, and then out into the meadow again, at top speed. There went Lady over on her head, rolling away like a ball, and the fox cub snarled and threw itself on top of her, rolling around and around as well.

Suddenly both animals sat down on their tails and began to lick their paws. They were tired of the sport.

There they sat side by side glancing out over the lake, at peace with the world, both of them.

"This is the time that fox cubs separate from their mother," whispered Father. "The cubs are on their own now, and that's probably how this one's come across Lady. It must have wanted some company again."

"But aren't dogs and foxes enemies usually?" asked Torris.

"Not always, and certainly not when they're as young as these," said Father. "They haven't learned to be enemies yet."

Torris thought this over.

It was exactly the same as what Grandmother had read out from the book of sermons, about the lion and the lamb grazing together. Perhaps all the creatures were just cubs then?

"Suppose Lady goes along with the fox cub now," he said.

"She almost certainly won't," said Father. "I think she's more likely to try to get the fox cub home to us. We'll see."

They sat quite still and waited. It began to grow cold, but they wanted to see what the two animals did. And at length Lady got up. She wagged her tail and trotted off toward the farm. The fox cub followed a short distance.

But then it sat down on its tail and would go no farther.

"Woof, woof," encouraged Lady.

The fox cub said nothing—just sat.

Lady remained standing, waiting and wagging, but it was no use. The fox had probably been taught by its mother that humans were not to be trusted, and it would not go over to the farm.

Then Lady raised her snout toward the evening sky and howled sadly.

"Uhu-u-u-u! Uhu-u-u-u!" she said.

"Ack, ack, ack!" replied the fox, with a hoarse, high-pitched voice. But it did not move.

And at last Lady realized that there was no hope of getting her new friend to come. She turned tail and padded off to the farm. She was hungry and wanted food.

"Yes, come on then, Lady!" called Torris.

Lady halted a moment when she heard his voice. Then she caught sight of Father and him and barked and raced as if her life depended on it. She had entirely forgotten her playmate.

But the fox cub gave a start when it spotted the humans, stood for a while looking, slant-eyed and curious, sniffing with its pointed snout. Then it ran in a zigzag back to the wood and vanished among the trees.

"Did you see the fine white tip of its tail?" said Torris. "How strange that all foxes have that white tip."

"You surely know that it's because Grandma threw a blob of cream at it when it was about to steal one of her chickens," said Father, laughing. "That's what the fairy tale says!"

7

Mikkelina Gets into Deep Water

The frost came to the hills.

It began with hoarfrost on the meadows. The yellow grass in the yard was white every morning, and the thin ice on all the puddles crunched dryly underfoot.

Then the little streams began to freeze, Bard's Lake next, and finally the river as well.

Torris noticed it one morning when he came out on the doorstep.

He didn't know at once what it was, but only that something was different, and he remained there, looking and listening.

Then he realized that everything had grown quite still. The river no longer roared. The cold had stopped its song. He went into the kitchen, where Mother was busy attending to Little Marit.

"The river is frozen, Mother," he said.

"I know," said Mother. "Today we'll shut out the cold."

Torris knew what that meant. He remembered from the

autumn before, and it was, in a way, a happy day, even though there was quite a bit of hard work to it.

They first plugged the walls with moss, which they had gathered on the moors. They dampened it slightly, to make it soft, and then poked it firmly in between the wall timbers, in places where there might be cracks. Torris was clever at this work, as he had such small, slim fingers.

Afterward Mother and Grandmother hung wall rugs behind all the beds. Grandmother had woven most of them. They were thick and fine, with lovely patterns in many colors, and they made it warm and cozy.

Finally they brought down the big sheepskin rugs, which had been hanging over a beam in the attic. Some of them were to be used in the sleds. But the nicest, sewn firmly onto woven rugs, were for the beds. The one Torris and Bard had was one of the softest, and even if it was bitterly cold at night, they never felt it under their rug.

They carried all the skins outside and beat them on the frosty grass. Afterward they were hung up to dry on the beam above the hearth. For Little Marit's cradle Grandmother had woven a beautiful little rug, which she sewed onto a fine white lambskin. Little Marit was going to sleep like a princess.

"That's as it should be," Grandmother said, rocking her on her lap. Surely that's not much to do for my namesake."

And then the job was finished.

There was still a great deal to do outside, however, before they could face the winter confidently.

All the winter wood that they had carted to the farm in the springtime had to be sawed and chopped. Father and Grandfather stood day after day sawing with the big timber saw. Swish-swish-swish sounded from out there in the yard. And afterward Grandfather did the chopping, while Father and Torris carried the logs into the woodshed and stacked them.

The wood that did not go into the shed was laid alongside the wall of the barn. This would be put to good use in the spring and summer, when it had dried out in the sun.

"Oh, but, Father," said Torris, "if we go on like this, cutting and cutting, there soon won't be any wood left in Broad Valley."

"That's a long way away," said Father. "New trees shoot up all the time, and where we have chopped them down, we can clear and cultivate. Besides, it's easier to keep wild animals away when there's open space around us."

"But what about the wood up there on the mountainside?" Torris asked.

"It shall stand," said Father. "It protects us against storms, and against landslides and avalanches."

But they didn't need to worry about avalanches yet. So far they hadn't had so much as a snowflake. The days came and went with only hoarfrost and a deep, cloudless sky.

"I wish the snow would come soon," Torris said at last. He was looking forward to getting out his skis and the little sled Bard and he used to ride down the fields on.

"Take it easy," said Grandmother. "We'll have more than enough snow this year."

"How do you know that?" asked Bard.

"I see many signs of it," replied Grandmother. "In the first place, the rowans were so plentiful in the autumn, and that's a well-known sign. And, besides, there are the squirrels."

"The squirrels?" asked Torris and Bard.

"Yes, haven't you noticed how they've been hiding their food this year?" said Grandmother. "I've never seen them fastening their cones so far up the pine trunks."

"Yes, but why?" asked Torris.

"So that their food won't be covered by the snow," said Grandmother. "The little animals know that there will be heavy falls of snow, and so they must see that their cones are easy to find well up the trunk."

Torris gaped. He couldn't understand how an animal could know things like that.

"To be sure, you and I don't understand this kind of thing," said Grandmother, shaking her head. "But the animals do. They feel it inside them, and they're never wrong."

Bard was already on his way out to Father and Grandfather with the news.

"There's going to be a lot of snow!" he yelled as soon as he reached the doorway, almost as if he expected the snow to start coming down in bucketfuls there and then.

The men stopped sawing.

"Does Grandmother say so?" Father asked.

"Yes," said Torris, who was following Bard. "Then there will be," said Father. "I'd better have a look at the boathouse. Some of the roof timbers are rotten and will give way if the snow gets too heavy."

"We'll go down there today." Grandfather nodded. "May as well do it now as later."

"As you wish," said Father.

They loaded one of the sleds with beams and a pile of birchbark. Blakken pulled the load down to the waterside. The boys and Lady ran along behind, and when they were halfway there, Mountain Wind came trotting up and wanted to join them.

The reindeer had grown so fond of company that he wanted to follow the boys wherever they went.

"All right, so long as you take care he doesn't run out on the ice," Grandfather said.

"We can tether him," shouted Torris. "There's rope in the boathouse."

When they got down, Father and Grandfather began to tear away the turf and the rotten rafters from the roof. Torris tethered Mountain Wind to a bush with a long rope, and then the boys amused themselves sliding on the ice.

They were allowed to when the men were there. The ice

had become fairly thick. It was only at the mouths of the streams that it was thin and dangerous, but they knew this.

Lady frisked about, sniffing her way over to a heap of stones. A weasel was sure to live there, for there were so many of them at the water's edge. She lay down on her belly with her tail up, sniffing at a hole. Then she began to dig, sending up a shower of earth and gravel.

Torris and Bard went across to see if she found anything.

A little head popped up from the top of the pile.

Lady did not see it. She just went on digging away at her hole, and it looked as if the weasel sat up there saying, "Yah, boo! You won't catch me!"

Torris and Bard roared with laughter, and the little teaser slipped down among the stones. But immediately afterward it popped out somewhere else, and now it began to insult Lady. It hissed and spat and was as furiously angry as only a weasel can be.

Lady heard it and looked up.

"Woof!" she said in astonishment.

She had not expected to see the animal up there. Then she took an enormous leap to get hold of the cheeky thing. But it was gone, only to reappear a moment later out of another hole.

"It's no use, Lady," said Torris, laughing. "It's far too quick for you."

But Lady attacked once more, not willing to give up so soon.

When Grandmother came down to them with food, they seated themselves on a log by the sunny wall and were really snug and sheltered. The air had turned somewhat milder the last few days, and so there was no risk of their getting cold. While they sat chatting, Torris caught sight of something moving out on the ice.

At first he did not understand what it was. But shortly after he saw that whatever was moving had four legs and a long tail, and he tugged at Father's sleeve and pointed.

Father shaded his eyes.

"It's a fox," he said. "It must be a cub since it's running around there in full daylight. Sensible animals lie sleeping at this time of day."

They kept their eyes on the fox. It moved in zigzags toward the land, slid where the ice was glassy and smooth, got to its feet again, and scuttered on.

"It hasn't smelled us yet," whispered Grandmother.

"But Lady will soon get wind of it," said Grandfather. "The wind's blowing this way."

Lady was still busy chasing the weasel.

But suddenly she stopped and turned her head toward the water, lifted her snout in the air and sniffed this way and that, and then ran toward the ice and looked out over it. She finally caught sight of the fox and gave a loud bark that resounded among the hills.

The fox stopped abruptly and pricked up its ears.

"Ack, ack!" it replied briefly.

"Woof, woof, woof, woof!" barked Lady in return, leaping and jumping along the water's edge. But she didn't dare go out on the ice. She was afraid of the cold, smooth surface, which was so glassy in parts that she could see the water underneath.

"Father, I think it's Lady's friend," whispered Torris.

"It's not at all unlikely," Father answered. "If we sit as quiet as mice, it may perhaps come in to Lady."

They did as Father suggested and did not move. Even Bard managed to sit quite still, his eyes as round as marbles, his back straight as a ramrod.

The two pups barked to each other all the time.

Lady ran back and forth along the bank, ventured some steps out on the ice, but quickly slunk back with her tail between her legs. The fox cub came at full speed with its tail right out. It must have been a long way out when Torris first caught sight of it, but it would soon reach land, and Lady was nearly curled up with delight at meeting it again.

Then something happened.

Bard gave a sneeze.

It was no ordinary little sneeze. It was a mighty sneeze that echoed among the hills and caused Bard to tumble from the log.

The fox stopped short. It slid forward some distance on its bottom. Then it turned sharply and streaked along the shore, bounding away without looking where it was going, and plop, it vanished into an opening in the ice with a great splash.

"Oh, no, how awful!" exclaimed Grandmother.

"Help it out!" yelled Torris, springing to his feet.

Father and Grandfather were already on their way. Father had grabbed an oar and Grandfather a rope. The others ran after them as fast as they could.

But Lady was first to reach the opening.

She crouched down on her belly and crept cautiously forward, whining and barking in high, shrill tones. She must certainly have understood what a tragedy this was for her fox friend, since she herself was so afraid of the dark holes in the ice.

Then the fox's head appeared.

Lady whined even more shrilly and pawed toward it. She came very near to going through the ice herself.

"Come here, Lady!" shouted Father sharply.

Lady obeyed, and Father thrust her back to Torris.

"Hold on to her," he shouted. "I don't want two animals in the water."

Torris held on tight to Lady, while Father edged carefully toward the opening. The fox cub had gotten its forepaws up on the edge of the ice now, but its frantic threshings broke the ice under its paws. Torris could see from its eyes that it was terror-stricken. It threw its head about in all directions, trying to find a way out.

Father had now lain down on his stomach, with the oar crosswise under him. In this way the ice would not so readily give under him, and he eased himself carefully forward.

"Throw out the rope!" he shouted back to Grandfather.

Grandfather rapidly tied a loop at one end of the rope and threw it out to Father, who grasped it. With his other hand he grabbed the fox cub by the neck fur. And curiously enough, the cub took it calmly and let Father attach the loop over its head and under its forelegs.

"Pull up!" shouted Father. He himself took a firm hold on the rear end of the fox while Grandfather pulled.

And, at last, there stood the fox on firm ice.

The little animal first shook itself so that the water showered off it. Father grew soaking wet where he lay, but he did not worry about that. He eased himself backward toward the bank, dragging the cub after him. The fox cub had become so stiff and cold with the icy water that its legs would not carry it properly, but slid out in four different directions, leaving it lying on its belly, shivering from tip to tail.

"We'll take it home with us to the cow barn and let it dry itself out," said Grandmother.

"Oh, yes, Mother," said Father, laughing, "I think you'd gladly have taken the bear itself into the cow barn if need be. But we'll try."

He took a grip on the rope, drew the cub toward him, and lifted it up. But the little fox struggled against him as hard as it could. It snarled and snapped at Father's arm and behaved like the wild animal it was.

"Will you stop biting, you stupid thing," Father said, holding it firmly around its snout. "If you could only know how well we're treating you."

"Yes, if it had been Old John who had caught you, you'd have been sitting as fox fur on the barn wall before the end of the day," said Grandfather.

Father was not really worrying very much about the little fox teeth, which failed to bite through his thick jacket. He carried the struggling animal over to the sled. There he laid it down on a sack and let Grandmother and Torris look after it. Grandmother sat down and took hold of its head, and Torris lay across the soaking wet back to hold it still.

Lady jumped up on the sled as well, wagging and barking and leaping back and forth over her playmate. Then she began to lick the wet fox fur, and the cub grew calmer and lay still while Blakken pulled the sled up to the farm.

Mountain Wind was released and trotted along with them up the slopes. He pranced somewhat restlessly around the sled. He was upset by the rank smell of wild animal.

"It isn't dangerous, Mountain Wind," cried Torris. "It's just a young one."

Grandmother sat looking at the cub.

"It's a little bitch, this," she said.

"Oh!" said Torris in astonishment. He had imagined that the fox cub was male. This was probably because foxes are normally called by a boy's name, Mikkel. "But what shall we call her, then?" he asked.

"Why not call her Mikkelina," Grandmother suggested.

Yes, Torris thought that was a good name. He stroked the little fox's back and felt somehow that he would have to take even better care of her as she was a bitch.

"I wish I could recognize her once we've let her go," he said thoughtfully. "But that's impossible, isn't it?"

"I'll think it over," said Grandmother.

They reached the farm and got Mikkelina indoors.

But first Mother had come racing out, quite beside herself because she thought it was Bard who was lying there.

"Oh, thank heavens!" she said, laughing and crying at the same time. "I thought that Bard had gone through the ice—but it's just a wretched little fox."

"Wretched little fox!" said Torris, insulted. "It's Mikkelina, Lady's friend. Look at her shivering, poor thing."

"Mikkelina will be my friend as long as she lives," said Mother. "She's even welcome to my plumpest chicken if only I can keep my children."

She lent a hand to get the fox into the stable. It was so warm there that Mikkelina's fur would soon dry, and Lady was allowed to stay with her and keep her company. Lady was more than willing.

She stood with her head cocked while Father loosed the

rope around her friend and, as soon as she was free, began to dance around her, wishing to play.

But Mikkelina ran off to the darkest corner and tried to hide. She was, and remained, a wild animal. It was with Lady alone she felt herself secure, and she didn't venture out before the humans had gone and shut the door behind them.

They looked through a crack in one of the door boards and saw her standing listening and sniffing for a time. Then she shook her fur and began to lick her wet paws.

"How strange it was to pat a fox," Torris said when they were out again in the farmyard.

"Yes, it may well be the first and last time you'll do that," said Father, and went down to the boathouse again.

Some hours later, after Father and Grandfather had returned, they set Mikkelina free.

She was now fine and dry. Grandmother had been down to see her and had given her a little food, and as they opened the door, the cub poked its sharp snout out of the stable, looked cautiously around, and took the shortest way across the yard and up to the wood.

The boys and Mother and Grandmother stood on the doorstep looking after her as she slipped past.

"Oh, but look!" cried Torris suddenly. "Hasn't Mikkelina got a red spot on her neck?"

"Well, now, have you ever seen the likes," said Grandmother. "She must have gotten it down there in the stable. And that kind of paint is impossible to get rid of, even if it's scoured with sand!"

Torris glanced at her. He knew from her voice that she knew a little more about that spot.

And then Grandmother couldn't help laughing.

"You see, there was a pot of red paint in the stable," she said, "and so I mistook the paint for the clot of cream I should have thrown at the fox. Yes, I happened to plaster it with the brush, right at the back of its neck, where it won't be able to lick it off."

"Oh, Grandma!" cried Torris, throwing his arms around her, "now I'll be able to spot Mikkelina again among all the other foxes."

"That's just what I thought," said Grandmother with a smile, "for, of course, they've all got white tips to their tails!"

8

The Great Storm

Grandmother's forecast came true. There were heavy snowfalls that winter.

And it happened so suddenly.

One night, not long after the day they rescued Mikkelina, the snow began to fall very heavily. When Torris stepped out of the door the next morning, he found the snow lying nearly two feet deep, and he stood there a long time looking out, for it was strange how everything had changed in one night.

When he went to bed the night before, the whole valley had been gray, except for the white mountaintops and the frozen lake. Now everything was white—mountainsides, fields, and trees. It was beautiful.

Here and there tracks of hare and fox crossed the fields. He looked curiously at them. Nothing was more exciting than to follow the tracks of animals in the snow and see where they had gone.

He was looking forward to getting out his skis.

Mother and Grandmother were not quite so overjoyed. The snow meant much extra toil for them.

"But it's so nice and bright now," said Torris.

"Yes, that's right," Mother had to admit. "There's that much good about snow anyway—it brightens up the dark winter."

"And it makes the houses more snug," said Grandmother. "You'd better get your spades out now and throw plenty of snow up around the walls."

But spades were soon unnecessary for *that* work. In a few days they had such masses of snow that it reached halfway up the windows, and they had to clear it away to let daylight in. There was plenty of work for men and boys. They had to keep open the paths into cow barn and stable and barn, and to storehouse and well. Soon all the entrances looked like underground tunnels, where the snow cornices reached right up to the eaves. It was possible to walk straight on to the roof if one wished.

But they gave up clearing the farmyard itself. Finally they just tramped down the snow so that they had firm pathways over the drifts. Father and Grandfather were careful to dig in tall hay poles along the beaten paths; then they could see clearly where it was safe to go. It was wisest to keep within the limits of the little "street" of poles. If you placed a foot out in the deep snow, you could be sure of sinking up to your knees, and that was not so pleasant if you were carrying an armful of wood or a couple of buckets.

"Keep to the track!" they kept hearing Grandfather shout after the womenfolk when they came along with their milk pails swaying.

"Ugh, that snow!" Grandmother sighed and kept her balance as well as she could over the deep drifts.

The weeks went by toward Christmas, with good weather and bad weather in turns.

Sometimes it was still and fine, with the tracks like satin beneath their skis; at other times the snow was crusted so that they could drive the sled right down to Bard's Lake.

But some days it was so bitterly cold that they preferred to stay in the kitchen and get on with whatever they had to do.

Then Mother and Grandmother sat at their spinning and weaving, while the men attended to equipment that needed repairing, made new buckets and troughs and such things that they always required on the farm.

Grandfather was also busy with a lovely big corner cupboard. It was to have carvings on the doors and on top, flowers and leaves and delicate intertwining ornaments. Torris and Bard hung over him and could not understand how he managed to get it so smooth and even.

"You'll learn all right, in time," Grandfather said. "You could tie a twig-whisk, Bard, and Torris can try his hand at a wooden spoon."

He gave the boys what they needed. Twigs and linen thread for Bard, and a suitable piece of wood and tools for Torris, and then he showed them what they should do and helped them with their work.

Bard and Torris kept at it, with their tongues in the corner of their mouths, while Mother and Grandmother held their breaths. They were terrified that Torris, who was using a knife, might cut his fingers. But Bard chased them away.

"You're not allowed to look," he said. "They're Christmas presents."

"Yes, just keep away," Grandfather said, smiling.

And so the two women had to get on with their own work, and the whisk and the spoon took shape and were finished without mishaps. There was just a little nick in one of Torris's thumbs, which he got as he was cutting out letters and the year on the handle of the spoon, for it was rather difficult. But with some help from Grandfather he got it at last to "M.B.D.," which stood for Marit Bardsdatter, and the year 1848.

It looked rather fine. He decided to make one for Mother also. Perhaps it would be even finer.

Bard hid the whisk under his bed, for Grandmother was to get it.

So time went by, filled with work and pleasure. Father and Grandfather were out at the wood cuttings when the weather was good enough, the boys went out on their skis or shoveled away snow, and Mother and Grandmother began to prepare for Christmas.

The days grew shorter and shorter.

The light was not really strong until quite late in the forenoon, and by milking time it was pitch dark. All work had to be cleared up during daylight hours, at least whatever had to be done outside. And one day, as they went across the farmyard, Grandmother halted and stood looking up at the mountain, listening.

"Today we must take in plenty of wood and water," she said, "for there's a storm getting up. I can hear a humming in the mountains."

Torris and Bard both listened as well.

Yes, there they heard it, a low, steady sighing as if from a waterfall far away. Torris had heard that sound before and knew it would not be long before the wind reached the valley—strong wind.

He ran in to Mother.

"We're going to have a storm today," he cried. "There's a humming in the mountains."

"Oh, no, are we?" said Mother, looking anxiously out of the window.

Mother had been born down in the village and could never get used to the violent storms up here in the hills. She went over to Little Marit and tucked her in better, as if she expected the blanket to be blown off her child any moment.

"Don't be afraid, Mother," said Torris. "We'll take in heaps of wood for you, so we won't get cold."

"Thank you, Torris my boy!" said Mother, stroking his hair. "As long as I've got you all safely indoors, I won't be frightened. I hope Father and Grandfather come home soon."

They did.

The two men had also heard the humming of the wind, and they knew that the storm could come as if suddenly let out of a bag. They were home just before midday and at once set to work making everything secure, as they always did when storms were expected.

Anything loose that might blow away was brought inside. All doors and windows were securely fastened, and wood and water to last for twenty-four hours were carried into the passageway and kitchen. Lastly Grandmother brought in food from the food store, enough for a day or two if need be, and then everything was finally ready.

Torris, meanwhile, kept going out to the doorway and looking toward the mountains.

Oh, yes, things were really happening up there now. Drifting snow swirled in gray-white clouds from the summits and all along Bard's Ridge, and the roaring was deeper in tone, like the rumbling of thunder. It would not be long now before the storm broke. He ran down to Mountain Wind in the cow barn.

"You mustn't be afraid," he said, and put his arms around the reindeer calf. "It is your first storm, but there's nothing to be scared about. It just roars a bit, but you'll be all right here."

Mountain Wind thrust his muzzle into Torris's hand. He probably didn't know very well what it was all about and just thought it was nice that the boy had come to see him. But Torris noticed that some of the sheep were restive, and the big bull stood rumbling and rolling his eyes.

"We'll be back again at milking time," said Torris comfortingly, and clapped the great beast. Then he ran out and shut the doors carefully behind him. The wind blew icily through his clothes as he crawled across the drifts, and he hurried into the cozy kitchen.

"The big bull's growling," he said.

"Oh, yes, the animals know what's coming, all right." Grandmother nodded.

Shortly after midday it grew dark—much earlier than usual.

Torris sat down on the bench beneath the window and watched the gray clouds piling up between the mountains. They sank lower and lower and hid the valley, first the mountainsides, then Bard's Lake, and finally the wood.

Soon everything had vanished. He laid his head on his arm and watched how the storm took the snow from the sky and the snow from the ground and swept it along with it. Now he couldn't even see the cow barn, only the gray-white snowstorm thundering past the windowpane.

"Ow! It's as well we're all indoors this evening," said Mother, who was standing behind him with Little Marit on her arm.

Little Marit prattled happily making all sorts of noises that only Mother understood. She was the only one who didn't care a bit if it was stormy or calm, so long as she was well fed and comfortable.

"Yes, we'll take very good care of you," said Mother, walking back and forth over the floor and rocking her.

"Come, now," said Grandmother. "Put the child in the cradle and sit down. The roof won't blow off the house."

Mother put Little Marit down and tucked her in well.

"All right." She sighed and went and sat down with the others.

But she was as nervous as an animal.

Every time a blast of wind caught the house, she started and glanced quickly at Little Marit. And when a sudden hard gust struck the wall, she gave a short, frightened cry.

"It was nothing," said Father, comforting her. "Just a broken branch. But you womenfolk are not allowed to go alone to the cow barn this evening," he added.

"Ah, no," said Mother.

Grandmother said nothing.

She had gone up and down the farm for the greater part of her life now. She could go blindfolded if need be and still make straight for the cow barn door.

"Hmh," was all she muttered as she glanced at Father.

There was silence once more for a time, while they listened to the storm. It raged so that the walls creaked and the smoke blew back down the chimney.

Father raked up the embers into a heap and placed a new log on top.

"The drift will give way tonight," he said after a time.

"Oh!" said Mother, and looked toward the window in a fright. She was terrified of the big drift. It lay huge and ugly up in the pass and could break and crash down at any time. When the drift lay so threateningly, the boys were never allowed to go that way. The avalanche it made when it broke loose had been known to go all the way down to the lake.

"Take it easy," Father said with a smile. "You know the farm is perfectly safe. I'm only saying it so that you won't lose your head completely when you hear it coming."

"Yes, if we hear it at all," said Grandfather. "There's such a din going on that the avalanche may have gone for all we know."

"I wish it had." Mother sighed.

They had found different jobs to do and were waiting for milking time. They would have liked to get it over and done with at once, but the cows had to be milked at the usual time, no matter what else was happening.

After a while Grandmother got up. She walked about for a bit, looked at Little Marit, asleep in her cradle, and glanced out of the dark window.

"Oh, no," she muttered, and walked toward the door.

Torris looked after her. He noticed that she had put on her milking clothes and head kerchief. She went into the passageway, but he did not say anything, for he thought that she was just getting ready and would tell them before she left.

But after some minutes had gone by, Grandfather had a sudden thought.

"Where is Grandmother?" he asked, looking around.

"I think she's busy getting ready," said Torris. "She went out into the passage. Maybe she's in the pantry."

Grandfather had a look. Then he turned and went through the kitchen into the bedroom.

"She isn't here, is she?" he asked, looking all around inquiringly.

"Isn't she here?" asked Father.

Mother stopped her spinning.

"Gracious," she said, "Grandmother surely can't have gone out alone?"

Grandfather went out to the pantry again.

"Yes, she certainly has," he cried. "The pails are gone."

They looked at one another.

Father leaped up.

"Oh, have you ever heard the like," he muttered, grasping the storm lantern that hung beside the door. He took a spill from the hearth and lit the thick tallow candle that was always ready in the big lantern. Grandfather threw on his jacket at the same time and stared out through the window.

"It's pitch black," he muttered, and ran to the door. "*Marit!*" he roared into the storm.

There was no reply.

"Hurry!" he shouted to Father. "It's a real hurricane outside."

Torris sensed from his voice that he was really afraid,

and he felt a chill prickling down his spine. When Grand-father was afraid, it was serious.

The two men ran out. The door banged shut after them, and Mother and the boys hurried over to the window and pressed their faces against the pane. The driving snow swept past in a horizontal stream outside, as solid as a wall, and they just caught a gleam from the lantern before it vanished in the dark.

"Oh, mercy on us!" said Mother helplessly, and pressed her hands to her bosom. "Maybe I should go after them and help?"

"No!" said Torris loudly. "You're not allowed to."

Mother looked at him, a little uncertain.

"No, Father and Grandfather won't allow it," said Torris.

"No-oh, I suppose I'd better not," murmured Mother.

Bard looked in amazement from her to Torris. Mother had listened to Torris and had done as he said, just as if she were a little girl and he was a grown-up man.

"If only they find her!" muttered Mother over and over again as she stared out of the window, where there was nothing at all to be seen.

The two men had found the right path. Father went first with the storm lantern, and Grandfather came close on his heels, with a firm grip on Father's shoulder.

"Here are the poles," Father yelled. "Take care you don't step outside them."

"Don't worry," Grandfather yelled back. "Do you see any tracks?"

"No, they've been filled in," shouted Father.

Everything was covered over in an instant. The lantern,

too. The snow stuck to the thick glass sides so that it couldn't throw its light more than an arm's length. Father had to walk bent over to pick out the way from pole to pole. Only their tops stuck up above the snow, and it was not easy to find them in the faint light.

From time to time they stopped and shouted.

But they neither saw nor heard anything of Grandmother.

A human voice did not carry far in the roaring storm. It was as if Father's and Grandfather's voices were cut off in the blasts of wind and vanished into the night. The farmyard was a swirl of white, with nothing to be seen in any direction—and Grandmother had not even had a lantern with her!

"She may have wandered right out into the fields . . ." muttered Grandfather to himself, peering helplessly into the dark. "Yes, that she may."

He knew what sort of impossible things a mountain storm could do, and he knew that nobody should ever go out alone in such weather. Grandmother ought to know that, too.

"Oh, but women!" muttered Grandfather, brushing the snow from his face.

They were now on top of the huge drift that lay right across the yard. Here the wind raged so fiercely that they could actually feel the drift moving beneath their feet.

Whee! A storm blast nearly swept them off the track. They bent double and clutched the nearest pole with both hands. It was almost impossible to draw breath so long as it lasted, no matter whether they turned their heads into the wind or away from it.

They waited there until the wind slackened somewhat.

Then they both bellowed. And suddenly they heard a feeble sound nearby.

"Hello!" shouted Father, shining the lantern around him as well as he could. "Are you here, Mother?"

"Ye-es," came the reply from somewhere in the dark. "He-ere!"

Father and Grandfather threw themselves down on their knees on the track. They held out the lantern in the direction the sound came from.

"Where are you?" yelled Grandfather again.

"He-ere—help me up," they heard, just to the right of them.

And there they caught sight of something moving. It was a bit of Grandmother's fluttering kerchief. She lay on her bottom in the deep snow, with only her head and arms and boots sticking up.

"No, did you ever!" shouted Father, brushing the snow away from her face. "Are you all in one piece, Mother?"

"Yes, yes, just get me out. I'm stuck!" shouted Grandmother.

Father and Grandfather nearly laughed with relief.

But now they had to get her up, which was not easy, for the snow had packed her in really tightly. They first had to scoop away the snow with their hands. Then each of them took hold under Grandmother's arms and pulled for all they were worth. And at long last there she was safely on the track, as white as the whitest snowman.

They both held on tightly to her.

"Can you walk, Mother?" roared Father, shining the light on her face.

"Yes, I can," gasped Grandmother, "but I lost both pails. I'll have to look for them."

"Oh, no, womenfolk!" howled Grandfather. "You're going in, you are, and right now."

They held her between them and balanced their way back carefully. And that was none too easy, either, for the wind got hold of Grandmother's skirts from beneath and very nearly whisked her right up into the air once or twice. But they hung on to her arms, and at last they got her along to the doorstep and into the warm kitchen.

There she was met with such joy, as if they hadn't seen her for several days.

Grandfather scolded mildly and happily, Mother bustled about finding warm, dry clothes, the boys babbled out questions, Lady barked, and Father brought warm milk.

There sat Grandmother, quite bewildered.

"But the pails," she said, shaking her head, "the fine, new pails!"

"Never mind the pails," said Grandfather. "They'll turn up in the spring. But how could you think of going out alone, and without the lantern?"

"Pooh!" snorted Grandmother. "Shouldn't I know my own farmyard without a light?"

"Oh, yes," Father said with a laugh. "We saw that much!"

But then Grandmother suddenly grew serious.

"You're right," she said. "I'd never have thought it possible to get lost in one's own yard. I was scared. And I've hardly ever been so glad to get into a warm room."

Some time later that evening, after Father and Grandfather had seen to the work in the cow barn, they gathered around the hearth as usual. They sat chatting about storms in the old days and about happenings they could remember.

Torris and Bard lay stretched on a sheepskin on the floor. It was exciting to hear about the time Broad Valley had been shut off by a storm for several weeks—and other stories of that kind.

Grandfather placed another pine log on the fire. It flared up with blue and yellow flames and warmed them so much that they had to move their chairs farther off.

"Do you remember the time that . . ." Mother began, but abruptly she sat up and listened.

The others looked at her and listened, too. Lady pricked up her ears and crept with her tail between her legs over to Grandmother. And now they all heard it.

The storm had taken on a deeper note outside. It rose in strength to a level roar, the flames flickered on the hearth, and the house shook slightly. It lasted only a short time. Then all was still. But Mother had found time to dash over and snatch Little Marit up from the cradle.

They looked at one another.

"There went the drift," said Grandfather.

"Thank goodness!" said Mother, and sank down on a chair. She held Little Marit firmly.

Father went over to her, took the child from her, and laid it in the cradle.

"There you are," he said with a smile. "The house is still standing."

"Yes," said Grandmother with satisfaction, "it's a good thing we got rid of that awful drift before Christmas. And thank heavens I wasn't lying out in the yard with my legs in the air right now!"

9

Torris Follows Animal Tracks

A week before Christmas a period of fine, calm, mild weather set in. The snow firmed up and grew easier to walk on; the valley seemed to level itself out and help to make the work of Christmas preparations easier.

It was now possible to run up and down the farm bringing in wood for Christmas. Father could drive safely to the village and collect household goods; Mother and Grandmother could dry the washing in the sun and wind and could shake out rugs and skins in the snow as much as they wished. These were days filled with lovely smells, activity, and fun.

Darkness fell early in the evenings. But that did not matter very much, for there were so many delightful things to do then as well.

Torris and Bard were allowed to join in the work of making fine new tallow candles. They needed many, both large and small—and some especially good ones with three branches to stand on the table on Christmas Eve. These were for Grandmother to make, for she had the skill of keeping the three wicks a suitable distance apart to give the candles a handsome shape.

The boys were allowed to make the thick, short candles that were to stand on the windowsill and shine out over the farmyard and show the way to their Christmas visitors.

They dipped the wicks up and down and up and down in the bowl with the hot, runny tallow, and it called for skill to get them round and smooth.

And then there were Christmas presents to be finished, and Mother needed help to hang up even more lovely rugs on the walls, and then the fire had to be tended under Grandmother's pot as she busied herself frying crullers in deep fat.

Oh, so much to do! It was the best week of the year.

Torris and Bard had to be chased to bed every evening and fell asleep to a wonderful smell, a mixture of soap-scrubbed woodwork and new-made candles.

But the brief hours of daylight were still the most important and had to be used to the full as long as they lasted.

The first thing Torris did in the morning, as soon as it was light, was to see if any fox had been there during the night. He laid out food behind the stone dike, a little dried fish and such, which he hoped Mikkelina would come and fetch.

The food was always gone in the morning, and sometimes there were fox tracks in the snow. He followed the tracks as far as he could. They went each time in a zigzag up through the wood in the direction of the huge fall of boulders at the foot of the mountain.

"That's probably where she lives," said Grandfather.

"But why doesn't she come here by day any more?" asked Torris.

"She's beginning to get grown up and cautious," said Grandfather. "But we'll take a trip in the spring and look for her. Maybe we'll see her then."

So Torris followed other tracks.

And one day when he was down by Bard's Lake to pick some juniper branches for Mother, he caught sight of new marks, not a fox's or a hare's, but deeper impressions made by hoofs going out over the ice.

Torris went down on his knees and looked at the tracks. They were like a cow's tracks, but smaller and narrower. It was a little elk that had gone there, most likely a calf that had been born in the spring. The line followed a direct course and vanished from sight far away over by the wood on the other side.

He stood for a moment in thought.

It was not so long since the animal had been there. If he moved fast, he might perhaps catch up with it. It was not so far across the lake, and the weather was fine—perhaps a bit colder today, but with clear sunshine. He took hold of his ski stick and set off.

But when he was a good halfway and had come into the shadow of the mountain, he felt it colder at once—not on his body, for he kept that warm with his skiing, but on his hands and in his face. He dug into his pocket for his mittens.

One of them was gone! He must have lost it when he stood looking at the tracks. Perhaps he had laid it down along with the branches of juniper.

Well, nothing to be done about that. He didn't bother

to turn now and race all the way back. He put on the one mitten and hurried on. The elk tracks were clear in front of him all the time.

It was certainly a longer distance over the lake than he had thought. But at last he reached the edge of the wood on the other side.

Here the elk had paced a little back and forth to find the best place to go up. It was not difficult for Torris to see the way it had taken, for the marks were quite distinct in the deep snow. But, poor creature, it must have been

pretty hard going in the wood. Its thin legs had sunk far
into the snow.

Torris struggled on after it. It was rather steep, but after
a time he was over the first slope.

Here the wood lay more level. It was mainly small
birches and big, gnarled pines; in one place a tight clump
of spruce were growing, and it was there that the elk calf
had gone.

Torris stood stock still and listened.

Perhaps it was in there now. Elks often hid themselves
by making their way in among closely growing trees and
standing motionless so as not to be seen. He changed his
mitten to the other hand, which had grown very cold, and
went closer, step by step, slowly, not to scare the animal.

Only a few yards now lay between him and the copse.

There were some eight to ten trees, heavy with snow.
The lowest branches hung almost to the ground. Torris
saw nothing of the elk.

Had it lain down to sleep maybe?

Woodland animals liked to find themselves places to lie
under such low branches. Often a hollow had formed in
the snow close to the foot of the trunk where it was fine
and cozy to be. He glided on, step by step.

Hush, was that a sound?

Yes, there was something stirring. He took another few
steps, went down on his haunches, and peeped in.

And then he caught sight of it.

It was a young elk calf, just as he had supposed. It lay
there among the tree trunks and turned its head to look at
him.

Torris gave a start when he saw it. He sat there and
stared at it. In a moment the elk calf was sure to jump up

and vanish. It must have been very frightened when it saw him. He waited excitedly.

But how strange that it did not get up?

It just lay thrashing about and looking at him. Was it stuck? Yes, it must be. Otherwise, it would have been off long ago.

Torris arose and slowly went nearer. The elk calf struggled even more fiercely and rolled its eyes. It was scared, he knew, but he had to investigate, and so he remained a little way off, looking at it.

"Don't be afraid," he said softly. "You're the second animal I've found stuck. Mountain Wind was just a baby calf, and you're bigger, but I'll get you up, don't worry."

He squatted down and looked more closely, stretched his hand out slowly, and laid it on the elk's back. A shiver passed over its body, but it lay still.

Ah, yes, now he saw it. Three of its legs were visible, but the fourth was stuck in something or other under the snow. He changed his mitt over to his right hand again and began to dig. But he sat so awkwardly with his skis on that he couldn't get properly at it.

"Just let me get my skis off, and then I'll help you," he said, pulling one foot out of the toe strap. The moment he put his boot down on the snow, his leg disappeared to well over the knee, and he tumbled over, falling half across the elk's back.

The animal gave a start, and Torris was tipped backward, which made his leg sink in even more deeply, and when he tried to pull it up, it was firmly stuck.

"Ach!" said Torris in annoyance.

He tried to wriggle his foot, but it hurt. He felt something pressing tightly around his ankle. At the same time he felt something alive moving against the inner side of his leg. He shivered.

Was it an animal?

Then he realized it was the elk calf's leg that lay closely against his own and that it had moved.

If only he could manage to dig himself out . . .

But he was sitting so completely back-about. His legs were twisted on top of each other, with one knee across the other. Nor could he manage to get the other ski off. The only movement he could make without pain was to bend forward over the animal's back.

He did this and tried at the same time to dig with his other hand, but that was impossible. His arm did not reach so far backward. He tried to jerk up his leg. That, too, was impossible.

Torris looked about him. He did not exactly know what he was looking for; there must surely be some way or other of getting out of this. But there was no help to be found in the quiet wood.

Then Torris grew frightened.

It was no use shouting. No one would hear him. No one knew he was here. Mother and Grandmother thought he was gathering branches, and Father and Grandfather were working in the smithy when he left.

How long would it be before anyone began to search for him?

It might be a good long time, for when the grownups were as busy as they were at present, an hour would soon go by without their missing him.

He raised his head and looked out over the ice that he could glimpse between the trees.

The shadow of the mountain crept farther and farther over and would soon reach the other side of the lake. The sun was about to set. It was out only for a few hours in the middle of the day. Soon it would be gone completely, and it would become much colder. He could already feel the cold creeping in under his clothes, for he had not put on very much when he went out.

He lay forward across the elk's back and stuck his fingers into its warm fur.

"I hope they'll think about me soon," he said to it. "Then they'll begin to search for me, and then they'll find us and help both of us out. I'm glad you are so nice and warm. I don't mean to scare you."

The elk calf turned its head and looked at the boy.

Every so often it tried to struggle free, but it was no more successful than Torris. And so both of them lay still, while the sun vanished behind the mountain and the freezing mist crept in among the trees.

10

Bogga Finds a Red Mitten

A while after the sun had sunk behind the mountain, a sturdy woman came skiing along the side of Bard's Lake. She wore a long skirt, a thick jacket, and a knitted kerchief, and on her back she carried a knapsack of birchbark full of good things.

It was Bogga.

She had a day off, as was her custom, to take a visit to Bard's Farm before Christmas, and she needed it, too, with all the hard work they had been having for so long down at the manse. Now she pushed her way along, at a steady pace that brought her on her way remarkably quickly. She had had a fine run up in the sunshine and went humming along, enjoying herself. She would soon be halfway, where the track branched off to Bard's Farm.

Then she stopped suddenly and looked down at the ice.

Before her lay a red mitten and a little heap of juniper branches. Bogga lifted the mitt and looked at it.

"So, so," she said, "a boy's been here, and he's lost his mitten. I just wonder . . . ?"

She looked around her and caught sight of the ski tracks.

"So, so," she said again. "He's gone on skis over the ice. And an animal has gone there, too. What am I to make of it?"

She stood for a moment thinking. Then she continued talking aloud to herself.

"He hasn't come back the same way, and there are no more ski tracks here. So he must still be over there, and he must be alone, and it's probably Torris. I'd better go and look for him."

Thereupon she stuck the mitten into her pocket, turned her skis, and thrust quickly along the solitary ski track.

Meanwhile, Mother and Grandmother were busy cleaning the bedroom back on the farm.

"I wonder what's happened to Torris?" said Mother.

"Oh, he'll be along soon," said Grandmother. "Maybe he's busy looking for his fox."

Mother remained standing with the washing cloth in her hand, looking out of the little window.

"I think he ought to be coming soon. The sun's down, and he was just going to get some juniper branches for me."

"Oh, he easily loses all track of himself, you know," said Grandmother comfortingly. "Maybe he's already home and is down in the smithy with the men. We can go and see shortly."

And with that they were content. They were used to Torris's wandering here, there, and everywhere, and he always returned before it grew dark.

Meantime, Bogga had reached the other side of the lake and was standing looking at Torris's ski tracks.

"That's an awkward place he's gone up," she muttered, measuring the steep bank with her eyes.

"*Torris!*" she shouted so that the echoes rang about the hills.

No one replied.

"Well, well, it's just a matter of putting one foot in

front of the other and then I'll surely get up," chattered
Bogga as she lifted up her skirts. She took a firm hold on
her ski stick with the other hand and struggled her way up
sideways.

"That's just like him," she panted, "but I'm going to
find him all right, even if he's wandered up to the top of
Cairn Peak!"

But Bogga did not have to go that far.

As soon as she had reached the top of the slope and had
gone a little distance along, she caught sight of Torris. He
lay across the elk's back asleep. Bogga stopped and looked
at him, terrified.

"Torris?" she said in a low voice.

It was a very long time since Bogga's voice had failed
her.

Torris did not reply.

"My dear child, please answer me!" said Bogga. "You
can't be lying there asleep?"

Not a sound came from Torris, for that's just what he
was doing. He was asleep. He heard Bogga's voice from far
off and could not understand why she was asking, for he
must surely be allowed to sleep when he was sleepy and
lying so warm and snug.

But Bogga did not seem at all convinced that it was a
suitable place to go to sleep. She glided quickly over to
Torris and gave him a hard shake.

"Listen here, Torris!" she shouted. "You must not lie
there sleeping in the cold."

Torris opened his eyes briefly.

"I've found the elk calf," he muttered.

Then Bogga threw herself down beside the boy. She did
not take off her skis. She realized that there must be some

dangerous knot of branches under the snow, which had caught Torris and the elk calf. She knelt on her skis and dug till the sweat poured from her.

"Torris!" she shouted again and again. "You've got to wake up now. I'll get you loose and then we'll run. Wake up!"

"Mmh," was all Torris muttered.

Bogga shook him firmly. She had placed her knapsack on the snow.

"What do you think I've brought for you?" she shouted. "New-made crullers!"

"Mmh," muttered Torris again. He was usually very much awake when there was talk of Bogga's crullers.

"And do you know the funny thing I saw on the way?" panted Bogga as she dug deeper. "I saw a fox with a red spot on its neck. Have you ever heard the likes!"

"It was Mikkelina," said Torris drowsily.

"I'll soon have you free," shouted Bogga. "Can you move your foot? Wake up, Torris!"

"I want to sleep," said Torris, thrusting his fingers more deeply into the animal's fur.

Bogga wiped the sweat from her face and wondered what she could tell the boy to get him properly wakened.

"Do you know what!" she shouted. "I've been allowed to have the little girl with me, the orphan child, you know. You can't believe how good she is."

Torris was still not interested.

But then Bogga took a grip of his shoulders and gave him a really good shaking.

"Now you're being really wicked," she said, making her voice harsh. "Do you wish to make your mother sad and have her cry for your sake?"

At last life came back to Torris. He raised his head and looked at Bogga.

"Why should Mother be sad?" he asked.

"But my dear child, don't you know you'll freeze to death if you remain lying here? We have to get you home."

Torris looked about him in confusion.

He had been so far away. He had dreamed so many things he could not clearly remember. And all those things Bogga had been saying about Mikkelina and the orphan child—he did not know for sure if they were part of the dream as well. But that Mother should cry?

He supported his arm against the elk's back and half rose.

"I didn't know I was asleep," he said.

"No, you wouldn't know," said Bogga, with her head well down in the snow. She was digging around his boot. "Are you cold, Torris?"

"Yes," said Torris, for now he really was freezing. He had not noticed it while he was asleep, but now he felt himself quite stiff. He could hardly manage to talk.

"Your foot is free," gasped Bogga, getting up on her knees. "Can you move it, Torris?"

Torris wriggled his foot carefully one way and the other and nodded.

"But it's so queer. I can't feel myself moving it," he said, shivering.

"Then we'll have to get some life into it," said Bogga.

She sat down and quickly undid one of her own boots and then Torris's boot. Then she took off her own warm sock, pulled it on his foot, and rubbed it good and hard.

Then she got both boots and skis on him and dragged him up. She was quite red in the face.

"Now," she said, taking a firm hold of him. "Now we'll go."

Torris tried, but his foot would not carry him.

"Come on," said Bogga, "hang on to me, and take one of the sticks."

"But the elk calf?" asked Torris.

The elk calf lay there watching them. It had not managed to get up. The long, thin leg was still stuck in the knot of branches.

"Your father'll fetch it," said Bogga. "And it can stand more cold than you. Come on now."

They managed to struggle their way down the steep slope and along the ice.

Torris looked at the broad level stretch and did not know how he would ever manage to cross it. He was cold, and his body felt so heavy.

"There's such a queer prickling in my foot," he said.

"Fine!" said Bogga. "That means life's beginning to come back to it. Try to step on it."

Torris put it down carefully.

"Ouch!" he said. It did hurt.

"Grand!" said Bogga. "It'll hurt for a bit, but afterward it'll get better."

She fished out some crullers for him, and Torris chewed them while Bogga thumped his back and tried to warm him up.

"My, Torris, the things you get into!" she said. "If you hadn't lost your mitten, so that I found it, and if you hadn't had the warm animal to lie on, I really don't know what might have happened."

"I tried to save it," said Torris.

"Then we might say that you saved each other," Bogga said with a smile.

"And you saved both the elk calf and me, because you found us," said Torris, and he, too, had to smile.

"Oh, but look! cried Bogga suddenly. "Isn't that a horse coming over there?"

Torris stared. Yes, indeed, it was Blakken coming at full speed down from Bard's Farm, with Father and Grandfather sitting on the sled.

"A-hoo-y!" shouted Bogga, waving her ski stick.

"A-hoo-y!" shouted Father.

And then it was just a matter of waiting for Blakken as he came trotting so fast that the chips of ice flew from under his hoofs.

That evening there was much to talk about around the hearth.

Torris sat wrapped up in rugs, with his feet on the hearthstone, and was as well as ever. Father and Grandfather had collected the elk calf and brought it into the cow barn. Now it lay together with Mountain Wind, and there was nothing the matter with it, except that it needed food and rest. They would keep it with them until the springtime, when the snow had begun to go from the fields.

Torris and Bogga had to describe all that had happened, and Mother didn't know what she could do to thank Bogga.

"And to think that here we were, believing all was well

and that there was no danger," she kept repeating. "Oh, no, just think!"

"But Father and Grandfather came," said Torris.

"Yes, we'd set off to look for you," said Father. "And just as we were wondering where to search, we saw you out there on the ice. Otherwise, we'd not have found you so quickly—that's for sure. There were so many ways you might have gone, you little rascal."

"Torris has learned his lesson now," said Bogga. "Suppose a wind had come up, Torris, and your tracks had been covered."

"Yes," said Torris as he thought the matter over. Then he smiled and looked across at Grandmother. "Grandma and I have both learned it."

"Oh, you tease!" said Grandmother with a laugh, slapping him gently on the cheek with her skein of yarn.

11

And It Came to Pass

While the bells rang out early on Christmas morning, a stream of people passed through the doors of the wooden church down in the village.

Mother and Father and Torris and Bard were also there. They had come down with Blakken and the sled, and they now stood outside the church waiting for Father to tie up the horse.

It was still dark, and Torris stood looking out over the valley where family after family came swishing along from all sides, with flaming torches on the sleds and ringing bells on the horses. The torches looked like shining eyes in the dark, and the sleigh bells rang so merrily.

In all the sleds, people were dressed in thick traveling furs, with the women and children so well tucked under the sheepskins that only the tips of their noses were to be seen. When the men stepped off the sleds, they looked like huge bears. They were so bulky that they could only go through the door one at a time.

Inside the church porch stood Mr. Nicolas, the minister, to greet each person as he entered.

His wig was splendid and newly coiffed, and his starched ruff stuck out stiffly. He greeted Father and Mother, who had Bard between them. Torris pushed his way in behind them, pulled his cap off, and bowed.

The minister ruffled his hair.

"Good day—er—er-er, well, what's your name again, boy?"

Torris looked up and grinned. He couldn't manage to answer. Father helped him.

"This is Torris. My elder son."

"Yes, of course!" said the minister, beating his forehead. "Torris Bardson, that's it. You were along with them and helped to find my sheep in the autumn, weren't you?"

So he remembered *that*. And finally he also remembered that Little Maid was a sheep and not his sweetheart.

But he would probably never remember his name before Torris was confirmed.

They entered the church and found themselves seats.

Bard, who was little, sat with Mother on the women's side. Torris sat beside Father on the men's side, right by the center aisle. Directly opposite him sat Bogga with a little girl. Torris recognized her. It was the orphan child. She sat squeezed tightly up against Bogga, looking a bit frightened. But when Bogga looked toward her and laughed, she smiled back.

"This is Tyri," whispered Bogga. "She's five years old, and now she's going to stay with me. She'll turn out all right once she realizes that she has a home where she belongs."

Torris nodded.

The church was now filled, and he looked about him.

The enormous tallow candles on the altar rail shone a

good distance down the rows, and he caught sight of Little John and his father and mother, whom they had come along with from Broad Valley. And there sat Beret and the other maids from the manse, and there, in the first row, sat the minister's wife with Gunhild beside her.

Gunhild had one arm resting on her mother's knee. She turned and gazed at Torris for a long time, and Torris looked at her. She was very dressed up today, with a black skirt and blue jacket with white collar. On her head was a little red bonnet with a ribbon tied under her chin. The light shone in her eyes, and she stared, unblinking.

He suddenly noticed that the church had grown very still, and he looked around him, startled. The bells had stopped ringing. The minister stood in the pulpit.

Oh, good heavens, was he angry because Torris had been sitting looking at Gunhild like this?

But he was certainly not angry. He looked very cheerful and nodded and smiled.

"A happy Christmas, one and all!" he said.

"A happy Christmas!" replied the congregation. And then the minister read the text for Christmas, which began: "And it came to pass in those days . . ."

It was about Mary, who gave birth to her child and laid it in a manger.

Torris liked that story. He was sure that the child had lain very snug and warm in the hay, for he himself lay in his bunk like that, and there was nothing so good as sleeping on new, fresh hay.

The only thing that was slightly difficult was the bit about the donkey, for he wasn't quite sure what a donkey looked like.

He pictured to himself Mary sitting on Blakken, and she looked like Mother and Joseph like Father.

That time Mary and Joseph went from Nazareth to Bethlehem was probably much the same as when they themselves went from Broad Valley to the village. And when Mary and Joseph could not find room at the inn, it was almost the same as when the folk from Broad Valley had come down to market and had to sleep in a barn because there was no room at the guest house.

More than once this had happened, and Father and Mother had put him, Torris, into a corncrib, where he lay safe and comfortable under Blakken's nose.

Yes—he could make sense of the whole story. He knew it almost by heart.

It was not so enjoyable when the minister reached the actual sermon, which took a long time and was hard to follow.

Torris sat looking at the flickering candles and at the pictures over the altar and the gleam of daylight as it came slowly seeping in through the tiny windowpanes. He looked at Father and Mother as they sat listening, and at the minister, who was talking rapidly and eagerly. He did all he could to keep awake.

But they had gotten up so early today to reach church in time. Now his eyes grew heavy. So did the other children's apparently. Bard, at any rate, lay outstretched on Mother's lap, and little Tyri slept securely in the crook of Bogga's arm.

Bogga glanced over at him and seemed to know how he was feeling. She put her hand into her pocket and fished out a cruller, which she passed to him, and he ate it up in small nibbles.

That helped, fortunately. It would have been dreadful for a big boy to fall asleep in church. Gunhild kept herself awake the whole time, he could see. But, of course, she lived right beside the church and so had surely been able to sleep for two hours more than he had. It was easy enough for her.

But Torris grew wide awake once more at the end, when the minister again said something he understood.

"We have much to be grateful for this morning," said the minister. "Now the light is strengthening, and we must give thanks that no lives were lost in the dark wintertime before Christmas. John from Torve came very close to losing his when he had to go for the doctor for old Ingeborg on the night of the storm. But he saved his life, praise be to God. And we must give thanks that the avalanches did not carry off people or animals. Let us hope that the wintertime after Christmas will be as merciful."

All were still.

Most of those who sat in church had been in some kind of difficulty, and Torris thought of Grandmother and himself and of what could have happened.

"Thank you that we found Grandma so quickly and that Bogga came and saved me so that I didn't injure my foot," he thought rapidly.

Then they sang the last hymn, and the morning service was over.

The bells rang out again, and they all went out into the churchyard and blinked at the sun that was rising above the mountain at that very moment. The church stood on the spot in the village the sun reached first. The horses and some sled reindeer stood dozing with their heads over their nosebags. But now they awoke and began whinnying and shaking themselves, making all their bells ring. The congregation walked about, wishing each other merry Christmas, and Torris bumped into little Tyri, who stood close to Bogga, almost hidden in her full skirt.

"I wish you a merry Christmas!" he said, just like the others, and took her hand. He did not know what made him do it, but he just wanted to because he had seen her that day in the autumn when she sat alone and frightened in the manse farmyard.

Tyri looked at him and curtsied, and Torris was quite embarrassed. It was the first time anyone had curtsied to him.

But Bogga put her hand under his chin and looked into his face.

"A merry Christmas to you, too, Torris!" she said.

Then they got back into their sleds for the return to Bard's Farm.

John and his father and mother drove in front, and they followed. They shouted to one another, about how lucky they had been with the weather, about when they should give their Christmas parties, about the guests they expected up in Broad Valley.

Bard was wide awake. But Torris grew more and more sleepy.

He lay so snug beneath the sheepskins that he scarcely noticed they were driving up through the snow-covered Black Gorge, where the men had to get off the sleds and help the horses. He lay thinking that he was now on his way home and that he was going to feed all his animals. They would get something especially good as it was Christmas Day. Mikkelina would get an old hen that had died.

He would sit up some moonlit night and see if he could catch sight of her, if he could manage to keep awake.

"Hi, Torris!" said Father, nudging him. "Do you see our eagle?"

Torris glanced up with sleepy eyes.

Yes, there it flew, high over Bard's Ridge, gliding around and around in wide circles. The sun glinted on the white stripes underneath the great wings, and Torris imagined, as he stared, that he, too, was gliding.

He saw the valley from above, with its snow-covered lake and fields and the two farms that looked like Gunhild's playhouse. They were so very tiny against the vast, sunlit mountain scape, but one of the farms was nevertheless his home, with cow barn and living room and a bedroom with hay and sheepskins in the bunk.

Down there in the wood Mikkelina slunk in and out among the trees, with a red spot on her neck; there Mountain Wind came loping across the fields with the snow flying from his hoofs; and there Lady came frisking with her tail curling across her back.

"Ooh, ooh!" called Mountain Wind.

"Woof, woof, woof!" yapped Lady.

"Yes, I'm coming now!" yelled Torris, stretching out his arms like the eagle's pinions to glide down to them—only to feel suddenly a soft reindeer muzzle against his cheek and an eager dog's tongue licking his nose. He awoke and found himself sitting in the sled in front of the doorstep at Bard's Farm.

"Where is it you're *coming?*" said Grandmother, who stood there to greet him. "You surely *are* here."

"Oh, yes!" Torris laughed and sprang out of the sled

furs. "I dreamed I was high up in the sky along with the eagle."

"You may very well have been up there, too," said Grandmother. "Nothing connected with Torris Bardson surprises me. Anyway, I do think we live quite high enough here as it is."

"Yes," said Torris, looking out over the valley with eyes already searching for more animal tracks. "We live high enough here, Grandma."